A LION'S PRIDE
THE SERIES

When A Beta Roars
(A Lion's Pride, #2)

By
Eve Langlais

Copyright and Disclaimer

Copyright © April 2015, Eve Langlais
Cover Art by Yocla Designs © May 2015
Edited by Devin Govaere
Copy Edited by Amanda L. Pederick
Produced in Canada

Published by Eve Langlais
1606 Main Street, PO Box 151
Stittsville, Ontario, Canada, K2S1A3
http://www.EveLanglais.com

ISBN-13: 978-1514109335
ISBN-10: 1514109336

Chapter One

Babysitting duty. The indignity of it burned—and in a way that no lotion could ever fix.

Hayder had better things to do on a Saturday night than babysit Jeoff's younger sister. Much better things. Important things. For example, his mane could have really used a hot oil treatment to keep it slick and hold pesky split ends at bay. He could have also played *Call of Duty* and worked on upping his prestige.

But no. Apparently being second in command didn't mean shit these days. Arik, the pride's alpha, said, "Guard the girl," to which Hayder replied, "Like hell." Not one to allow subordination—or pass up a chance at sport—Arik jumped over his desk, wrestled Hayder to the floor, wrapped him in a chokehold and threatened to have Kira shave his head if he didn't comply.

Not the hair! With such a dire threat hanging over him, Hayder agreed to the job.

The forced agreement meant he found himself outside a nondescript door, dreading the next few days or, gasp, weeks, if the situation didn't resolve itself rapidly.

Wanna go play. Such a sulky request.

His poor inner kitty didn't understand the concept of duty. It wanted to hit the farm that the pride owned on the outskirts of town. Acres and acres of wild forests, wheat-filled fields and teeming with wildlife. A perfect location for a bit of sport.

Not happening. He had his orders, and like

them or not—very not!—Hayder wasn't one to shirk his duties. Bitch and moan, yes, but in the end, he respected Arik's command—and feared Leo's moderating fist.

The pride's omega didn't believe in soft talk and coming to a mutual agreement by discussion. Leo smacked sense into a person because, as he explained, "It's faster."

Raising his fist, Hayder knocked on the condo door but didn't wait for an answer. Being the pride's beta gave him certain liberties, such as access to all the units in the building—a building owned and managed by, you guessed it, the pride.

Slapping his hand on the control panel alongside the door, he waited for the telltale click before turning the handle to open it. In he walked, uninvited, only to stop dead.

Almost literally, and with good reason, given a gun wavered in front of his face. Bullets fired point-blank never boded well.

However, the weapon wasn't the most shocking thing he faced. No, that was reserved for the possessive growl of his lion and the unwavering sureness that gobsmacked him when he caught the scent of the gun wielder. A woman. But not just any woman.

Mine. Our mate.

Uh-oh.

Like most shapeshifters, Hayder had heard of the so-called certainty that hit certain couples when they first met. The zing of awareness. The moment of recognition. Or, in his case, the slam and resounding clang of a door on a cell labeled Monogamy.

Argh. Not the dreaded M word.

A cowardly lion might have run away, but Hayder wasn't one to fear anything, especially not the short and trembling woman in front of him.

Barely reaching his chin with deep brown hair held back in a ponytail, she didn't possess a fearsome mien. On the contrary, everything about her appeared soft and delicate, from the silky smoothness of her skin and the long lashes framing the biggest brown eyes to her cupid's-bow lips, pursed and pink. She was also, judging by her scent, a Lycan.

Cats and dogs aren't supposed to mix. But tell that to his lion, who urged him to give her cheek a lick to say hello.

Uh, no. Somehow slobbering over a woman, armed with a gun, didn't seem appropriate. Introductions, though, might help.

"Are you Jeoff's sister?" he asked when she didn't seem inclined to speak. Nor did she lower her weapon, but he allowed it for the moment. The acrid stink of fear rolled off her and agitated his lion.

She fears. Feared him and Hayder didn't like it one bit.

"Who are you? What do you want?" Her words might have proven more forceful if they'd emerged less breathy and high pitched.

"I'm Hayder." He might have said more, like *I am the most awesome beta the pride could ever hope for*. He could have boasted he was a lion with a mane only slightly less impressive than that of Arik, the alpha king. He might have probably said something witty and flirty too, if she hadn't almost shot him!

Chapter Two

Bang.

Oh no. Arabella couldn't help but feel horrified. She'd almost shot the pride beta, but in her defense, it was kind of his fault.

Rewind a few seconds to how it happened.

Upon hearing someone at the door, Arabella fumbled the gun that had never left her side since Harry's death. No sooner had her mate died, leaving her an heiress with a sizable fortune, than the other wolves in the pack had come sniffing—and demanding.

Not interested. She'd made the mistake of jumping too young and too quickly into one relationship—a really wretched one—and she wasn't about to get herself dragged into another.

Her would-be suitors didn't care. It wasn't Arabella they wanted but the fortune she'd inherited and the power she represented as widow of the last alpha for the Northern Lakes Pack.

Say hello to the prize in a tug of war over who would next wear the title of alpha. Never mind her mourning period for her mate was far from finished. No sooner was the last shovelful of dirt dumped than Lycans were fighting over who would claim her, and according to rumors, once they mated her, the plan was to get rid of her.

A pity she wasn't in the mood to die. At only twenty-five, she had too much to live for. Only one problem. Saying no wasn't an option.

Step in her big brother, Jeoff.

"Come live with my pack," he'd demanded.

"I can't." While her brother meant well, he didn't have the numbers to take on the kind of war her old pack would wage in their quest to control her. However, while she couldn't bring that kind of danger to her brother, neither could she stay within the Northern Lakes Pack enclave, not unless she wanted to be forced to mate with whoever won the title of alpha during the next full moon.

It boiled down to a need for a stronger defense. A bigger pack who could handle the threat. Or, even better, "A lion's pride," Jeoff announced with sudden inspiration.

"What?" Surely she misunderstood. Everyone knew the felines and wolves tolerated each other at best.

"You need to ask for protection from the pride that runs my city."

"Are you insane?" she'd replied.

"Yes." Jeoff didn't even bat an eye as he admitted it. He also didn't listen to her protests as he made arrangements.

Stupid, over-protective jerk. How she loved her big brother, and truly, his idea was probably her best-case scenario.

Arik's lion group was known for its strength and numbers. Only an idiot would mess with it. Buried within its folds, maybe, just maybe, she could find safety. But Arabella knew better than to let her guard down. Hence the gun that she aimed at the intruder who entered the condo the pride had loaned her.

What does he want? Who is he?

The impressively-sized man standing framed within the doorway made her shake and for more than one reason.

For one, he'd just entered after a brief knock. Surely a person with manners would have waited for her to reply? Then again, he hadn't kicked down the door so that probably meant he had the right to be here. Could she trust him?

The expression on his face was anything but promising. On the contrary, he didn't seem pleased at all. Golden eyes widened as they took in her appearance and the wobbling gun. His lips thinned. The air practically crackled around them. She sucked in a tremulous breath, just a small one, and despite the pills she'd popped earlier, it took only one whiff for her allergies to act up.

Her sinuses jammed, and she knew in that instant the guy was a darned cat. Great. Just her luck that her brother, in his quest to protect her from her previous life, had sent her to live with a bunch of felines even knowing she was allergic to them. Usually she reacted to only the household variety and not the shifter kind, but tell that to her tickling nose.

The antihistamines she took failed her. Her nose twitched. She sniffed. It tickled more. She tried to hold it in. Tried to—

Epic fail.

Achoo!

It came out of nowhere, a massive sneeze that rocked her whole body. Whilst in its grip, her finger tightened on the trigger of the gun and caused a second explosion, not of the nasal variety.

Bang!

Oh dear.

"Holy fuck, lady!" The guy who'd introduced himself as Hayder yelled before he yanked the revolver from her loose grip. "You almost killed me there."

"Sorry." It was what she meant to say, but with her stuffy nose, it came out more like "Sawwy."

A frown drew his brows together in a line, and for a moment, she braced herself. She knew what that look meant. She'd angered him, and when women pissed off men, that usually meant a slap, or worse.

At least it did in her old pack. She knew within Jeoff's group, things were different, but since Arabella didn't know how it worked with cats, she prepared for the worst.

Shoulders hunched, head dropped so her chin almost touched her chest, she adopted the most submissive pose she could manage upright.

Instead of a cuff, Hayder—whom she knew from Jeoff's quick rundown was the pride's beta—turned his head and barked, "Nothing to see, you nosy felines. Go back to your rooms."

To Arabella's embarrassment, she found herself the object of craning scrutiny by more than a half-dozen female faces.

"We heard a gunshot," one stated.

"Who is that?" asked another.

"Who let the dog in?"

Hayder moved to block even more of the doorway, his bulky body providing a screen to hide behind as he addressed them. "None of your business who she is. As for what you heard, it was just a simple misunderstanding. Now shoo, before I tell Arik you're bored and in need of some kitchen chores. I hear the dishwasher is broken again."

That threat got the crowd scattering, all except for the beta, who entered the condo and kicked the door shut.

No audience? That couldn't bode well.

To give herself space, Arabella took a few steps back, but he wasn't interested in giving her room. Hayder flipped the safety latch on the gun, tucked it into the waistband of his snug jeans, and stalked toward her, golden eyes intent.

And scary.

For a second time, she couldn't help but take note of his appearance, in much greater detail this time. Tall, much taller than her five-foot-three frame, and wide, much wider than her chubby size-sixteen body— donuts might not solve the woes of the world, but they did provide respite.

She swallowed hard as his intimidating amber eyes locked onto her and wouldn't let go. It shook her, shook and tingled all her senses, just not in fear.

Unless I fear my attraction to him.

He exuded a wild and casual handsomeness with his long, tousled hair, a shade of light brown. The glimpse of muscles hugged by his snug white T-shirt proved distracting, but it was his lips, sensual lips pulled tight, that distracted her with an odd thought—*I wonder if they soften when he kisses.*

What a strange thought to have and for a man who appeared ready to throttle her.

His brows drew together in an impressive frown, and she cringed. It served only to knit them tighter, but instead of hitting her with a slap, he snapped, "Why are you shaking like a leaf in a windstorm?"

Like duh, because he was pretty darned

intimidating. She thought it, but didn't say it. Never speak the truth aloud. Another lesson learned in her pack. What she did reply was, "I'm sorry." Apologies, that was what men liked to hear.

Not this one.

"Sorry for what? The gun going off? That's not your fault. I should have known better than to just walk in, especially since you're here for protection. Although, if you're going to wander around with loaded guns, you might want to get something for your head cold so you don't accidentally shoot someone the next time you cough or sneeze."

"I don't have a cold. It's my allergies."

"What are you allergic to? Is it something in the condo? Did they forget to dust? Tell me what it is, and we'll get it replaced or fixed." All great offers if they were part of the problem. How to explain the truth?

He took a step toward her, and her nose tickled. She tried to hold it in, she did, but he kept getting closer, all the while hammering her for an answer so she finally blurted it out, "I'm allergic to cats."

That stopped him dead. His eyes widened, and not just because of her reply.

Achoo! And yeah, this time, while she didn't fire a gun, she might have done something worse. She sneezed on him.

Chapter Three

She's allergic to me!

If he'd thought himself stunned at the realization that the trembling woman was probably his mate, then it was nothing compared to his disbelief that fate thought it would be funny to pair him with someone who couldn't get near him without going into a sneezing fit.

And forget a petite ladylike sneeze. Nope. This woman might not stand taller than his chin, and she might present herself as the epitome of womanliness with her epic curves, but there was nothing delicate about the exhalation that came bursting out from her. It was also quite wet, which his inner feline didn't like at all.

But her embarrassment and red cheeks were quite cute and mollified his indignant cat.

Before he could say a word, she ran away from him.

She runs. We should chase.

Hayder almost did, but he refrained long enough that she returned, bearing a towel.

"Here." She offered the cotton fabric to him.

With a hint of a smile tugging at his lips, he took it to wipe at his face and shirt. He didn't especially mind a little bit of spit—and would dearly love to maybe wear some of her cream—but accepting her towel of apology seemed to ease her somewhat.

If only she would stop trembling and ducking her head. He could smell the fear rolling off her, and it irritated the hell out of him.

Surely she didn't fear him? Perhaps he'd entered a little abruptly, but still, he'd done nothing to deserve this level of trepidation.

When she didn't seem inclined to speak, he broke the ice, gently this time so as to not startle her. "Let's start over, shall we? I'm Hayder, the pride's beta. Arik sent me to guard you."

"Oh no. He really shouldn't have done that. I'm not important enough to warrant that kind of protection. Surely an important man like yourself has better things to do."

Yeah. He probably did, but he suddenly couldn't think of a single thing more important than the duty of keeping the timid she-wolf before him safe. Okay, that was a lie. He did know something more important—*What do her lips taste like, and how will she fit into my arms?*

Perfectly he'd wager. Just like she'd look even better naked on his bed. But he might be rushing things a little. He should probably first put her at ease—and invest in a pocket handkerchief, seeing as how she sneezed again, this time aiming away from his face.

"I don't mind guarding you." Forget what he'd thought a few minutes ago. Arik was right. Her protection was a priority.

"Surely they could send someone else. A man of your position shouldn't lower himself to babysitting me."

How dare she think so little of herself, never mind he'd entertained the same reasoning. "I don't mind doing it. You're Jeoff's sister. We might not be the best of buds, but he is a cherished ally of the pride. It's our pleasure to help him out." Oh, how Jeoff would have busted a gut to hear him lying so hard. While he liked and respected Jeoff, they had a rivalry that went back to college when they'd constantly vied for positions on sports teams—and the attention of the same hot girls.

"But by helping me, you're inviting trouble."

Trouble? His lion perked up. Trouble meant fighting. Which, in turn, meant fun. Bring it. "We can handle any trouble that comes our way."

"You don't understand. My old pack..." She trailed off.

"What about them? They won't dare mess with you here. The laws"—created centuries ago by some unknown entities, were something they all abided by—"will keep them in line."

"No they won't." She wrung her hands as she turned from him, and he almost reached out to reel her back, to tuck her against his chest and hold her safe. But she might not welcome such intimate attention quite yet. Give it a few minutes.

"The laws are the laws."

"To most. However, my old pack, they don't abide by normal rules. They thrive on violence. They make their own laws."

"If they break them, then they'll face the consequences." And yes, he might have sounded a little more gleeful than necessary. "Exactly what is the situation anyhow? I didn't get many details." Mostly because he'd spent most of the time after being given his orders bitching and moaning—in a manly way of course.

"They want me back."

"Well, they can't have you." It might have come out a tad more vehement than necessary.

She froze and shot a glance at him over her shoulder. "But they will try. I only barely escaped. Once my mate died—"

"You were mated?"

Turning away from him, he noted the roll of her shoulders. "More or less. Harry claimed me right out of high school."

"Harry." He rolled the name around on his tongue. "The name sounds familiar."

"He was alpha of the Northern Lakes Pack."

"He was your mate? But he was the same age as my da." He couldn't hide the incredulity in his voice.

"Yes, he was much older than me."

He winced as he grasped how his words might sound. "Sorry, I didn't mean to sound like a dick. I'm sure you loved him, and age wasn't a thing." A sudden flare of irritation, as well as an angry mental swish of a tail, left him confused. Why should he care about her previous mate? He couldn't expect the women he dated to be virgins. But it bothered him. The idea she might love another irked him. Or did she love him?

She made a noise. "Loved him? Hardly."

"But you were mated."

"Because he tricked me." She clamped her lips tight.

"How?" She shook her head, but he wanted to know, so he pressed. "How did he trick you?"

"I shouldn't speak ill of the dead."

But it wasn't anguish he sensed oozing from her at the subject she tried to avoid, more a dread. The fear had returned.

"Tell me what happened." He used a commanding tone, refraining a wince as her fear level spiked. But she spoke.

"As I said, Harry was several years older than me. On a visit to an aunt who lived in his pack, he met me. He decided he wanted me as wife and pursued me. I was young, stupid, and flattered."

"I am getting the impression he wasn't a great husband."

She didn't prevent the wry twist of her lips as she replied. "Understatement. But I accepted my fate."

The resignation in her tone made Hayder want to hunt down Jeoff and shake him then beat him for letting his sister suffer in a bad marriage. "Someone should have killed him. No one should ever abuse a mate."

His statement brought her around again so she faced him. "That's what Jeoff used to say all the time."

"So why didn't your brother kill him?"

"Because I wouldn't let him. Because he didn't have the numbers to face down the pack. Because he shouldn't pay for my mistake. And I'm glad I stopped him. In the end, Harry was killed, a victim of circumstance—also known as a hunter with a gun who saw a wolf and fired."

No one could have begrudged the petite woman the triumphant smirk, a hint of spirit hiding beneath the timid surface.

"Okay, help me out here. If the guy died, then why the hell are you in danger now? Since when does the widow of an alpha decide the next in power?"

"She doesn't. They're not looking to claim me just to become the next leader. They want me because of the fortune I inherited. Harry was rich. Stupid rich. I was his sole heir. When I wouldn't immediately pick a new mate, the fighting started. Everyone thought they had a claim. The only reason I made it out at all was because they were too busy fighting over who would get me. Since too many men stepped forward wanting a piece of the pie, they arranged a Lycan duel on the next full moon. Winner take all—me, the role as Northern Lakes Pack alpha, and the fortune."

"Wasn't there a contender you could have tolerated?"

No other male. His lion bristled at the very thought.

Calm down. Obviously none appealed since she'd chosen to escape. It mollified his lion for the moment.

"Perhaps, but…" She let her words trail off.

"But what?"

"See the problem is, while I might have handled a new mate, after all, I survived living with Harry, I wouldn't have lived long past the wedding. Rumor has it that, as soon as whoever claims me gets their hands on my fortune, I will end up dead because, as the pack beta said before locking me up, no one wants to keep sloppy seconds."

Ouch. The ugly insult had Hayder wincing. "That's harsh." He'd have to make a point to meet this so-called wolf pack beta and teach him some manners. His knuckles were well versed when it came to imposing civility.

Her nose wrinkled. "Harsh? Not really. I've heard much worse."

That didn't appease him. It just made his anger simmer hotter. He tried to change the focus on getting more details. "If this dude made you a prisoner, then how did you escape? Because I'm going to wager you weren't exactly given a ton of freedom to come and go as you pleased."

A small smile curved her lips, a tiny ray of sunshine that his feline self could have curled up and basked in. But it wasn't a smile for him. "Jeoff came to my rescue. He and a few friends actually hired a helicopter, rappelled to the apartment where they were holding me prisoner, and rescued me. I've been in hiding ever since."

"And you're convinced they won't let you go?"

"I know they won't. They'll do anything to get me back."

While she didn't elucidate what her old pack might do to get her back, Hayder had a general idea. "So we can expect them to come sniffing."

"More than sniffing. They will get rough."

He couldn't help a wide smile. "Really? You think they'll come poking around? Awesome."

"What do you mean awesome?"

"Awesome because we're a rough crowd too, especially the ladies in the pride. We also need plenty of exercise. Your old pack might think they can strong-arm or threaten us into giving you back, but guess what? That won't happen. I guarantee it."

Whether Arabella knew it or not, she was now part of the pride—and his.

And no one touches what's mine.

Rawr!

Chapter Four

If Arabella thought Hayder would keep her hidden away, out of sight from the pack that hunted her, she was wrong. The man seemed determined to flaunt her existence, or so it seemed when he insisted they go out to dinner.

Not happening. He might have somehow gotten her to spill her secrets, but she wouldn't give in to his newest request.

"Go out, as in present myself in public?" She shook her head. "I don't think that's a good idea."

"What are you talking about? It's a great idea. I'm sure you're tired of being penned in, out of sight. We'll check out a bit of the town. Grab some food. I'll bet you're hungry, and lucky you, I know a great steak place."

"I'm fine staying here. Really. And I'm not that hungry."

It might have been more believable if her stomach hadn't gurgled when he said, "You have to come. This place serves the most decadent brownies for dessert drizzled in a sweet, groan-worthy caramel."

"Chocolate and caramel?" Double whammy. Had Jeoff tattled about her weakness? It didn't matter. Hayder hit her hard with his tempting words, and her resolve crumbled. She slapped mental mortar on the cracks, trying to hold it together.

It might have worked if Hayder didn't play dirty. "They're the best chocolate brownies you'll ever eat. Warm from the oven, moist, velvety and rich on the tongue. It's accompanied by vanilla ice cream, not the store-bought kind. They make their own creamy version. Then imagine, gooey, sweet caramel sauce, zigzagged atop it. Utter decadence in your mouth."

It wasn't just the dessert that sounded like utter decadence. Stuffy sinuses or not, whatever vibe Hayder exuded wrapped her in a warm and relaxing cocoon, which, at the same time, proved invigorating—erotically so. His low, growly voice and chocolate promise took a sledgehammer to her remaining defenses.

Sultry seduction on two legs. Who could resist, not her, especially when he turned his smoldering gaze her way. Lions might not purr, but this man certainly did, and each syllable tickled across her skin arousing—

What was this? Arousal, and for a stranger?

How odd. And, no, she wasn't mistaken. Abused and wary didn't mean she was naïve enough to not recognize it. Once upon a time, she'd felt the same thing for Harry, but that changed once his true colors—and fists—emerged.

Don't remember. Stay clear of that dark past.

She needed to remain in the here and now. Here with this man, this very attractive man who took a step toward her, his hand raised and stretching out as if he would touch. His proximity triggered a deep trembling, and her lips parted as—

Achoo! This time she caught the impending explosion and aimed it away from the man.

Protecting him from her persistent sneezing, though, didn't stop his irritated utter. "I can't believe you're allergic to me."

"I'm sorry. Usually my antihistamine pill prevents this kind of reaction. Maybe you're more kitty than I'm used to?"

Too late, she realized how that sounded, and judging by the grin splitting his lips, he did too. "Oh, baby. I am a whole lot more *kitty*."

Nothing could have stopped the blush from heating her cheeks. Nor could she halt the quiver in her lower belly as his words stroked her. Staying close to him was not a good idea, and for so many reasons, and she wasn't insinuating the allergic kind. "Maybe you should go to dinner without me." Out of sight, out of mind, and maybe she could remind herself why she needed to steer clear of men.

"You think I'm going to leave you? Not likely. For one, as your acting bodyguard, that means you and me stuck together until the danger passes, baby."

"But what of my allergies?"

"We'll figure something out. Maybe the more time we spend together, the more your body will adjust to my scent. I refuse to have you allergic to me."

How determined he seemed. Why did he care?

Because he's ours.

What a strange certainty to have pop up out nowhere. Only it wasn't exactly nowhere.

You're back?

Arabella mentally queried, but her other side remained quiescent. But that didn't matter. She'd heard her. *My wolf isn't completely gone.* Although it had been a while since her cowed canine side had spoken.

How she'd missed her wolf side. Harry and the others had tamed the wildness from her years ago.

Not tamed, merely sent into hiding. Another quiet

thought. How nice to know her inner bitch wasn't gone forever, simply hiding.

Did this mean she could—

No. Better not to think it and jinx it.

A hand clasped hers, and the jolt of awareness sucked her from her thoughts as it struck all her senses with lightning strength. Every nerve ending tingled, sensations amplified. She sucked in a breath, and her first impulse was to pull away. However, Hayder wasn't letting go. On the contrary, his fingers tightened around hers, lacing them together as he tugged her toward the door.

"I—We   shouldn't—But—"   Half-hearted protests slid past her lips, none of them complete or coherent, not that he would have listened. He seemed intent on going to dinner, and she was coming with him whether she liked it or not.

Sneezing or not.

Achoo.

She managed to only let the tickle overtake her once in the elevator and ducked her head even as her cheeks heated at the growl that rumbled through him. She wasn't doing it on purpose. "I'm sorry."

"Would you stop apologizing?" he snapped.

She didn't want to anger him so she nodded and kept her head tucked low.

"And stop doing that. You're not some beaten slave. Hold your head up, baby. Tell me to fuck off."

The language didn't shock her and cause the O of surprise. It was his insistence she defend herself.

She shot him a wary gaze, waiting to see the challenging smirk. She knew how this worked. Tell her to do something, and then tear into her because she dared.

"There's those beautiful eyes," he teased. "Now keep them up here. I want to see you staring at my face. You're safe here. Especially with me. You can say what you want. Whatever you want. I would never hurt you."

He wouldn't.

Where did that certainty come from? So what if perhaps, thus far, despite their less-than-auspicious introduction, Hayder had shown her nothing but kindness? She didn't know him well enough to gauge if it was an act. She'd fallen for the lies before. "How do I know I can trust you? How do I know you won't turn around and hurt me when I do?" The words spilled from her, painful in their honesty, and shocking him into momentary silence.

"Because you can," was what he finally muttered.

"Of course I can," she said in a soothing, placating tone. Best to not antagonize him and call his word into question. He might seem sincere, but Harry seemed nice once upon a time too. *Don't fall for his charm. He'll hurt you too.*

How insidious her inner voice proved, cautioning and warning her not to trust so easily. Words were easy. Actions, though, proved much harder, and fists harder still. Honor was easier to break than maintain.

When the doors to the elevator slid open, Hayder, his hand still laced with hers, stepped in to a large lobby. Arabella couldn't help but stare. When they'd arrived earlier, Jeoff had smuggled her in through an alley at the back, not daring to have her brazenly come through the front doors.

"The longer we keep you hidden, the better chance we have of any trackers abandoning their hunt and leaving you

alone."

It seemed Hayder harbored a much different view. He showed no qualms at all. As nonchalant—and handsome—as ever, he dragged—and, yes, she dug her feet in and tried to stand still—her out onto the marble floor. The wide gleaming expanse boasted a polished mahogany reception desk manned by a security guard in a dark blue uniform. The rest of the floor space was overtaken by a lounge area carefully arranged with leather chairs and divans.

The vast area also contained a multitude of curious eyes, all of them focused on her. Noses twitched. Being the object of so many stares had her tucking in closer to Hayder. He draped an arm around her, tucking her into the comforting strength of his body, which had the unfortunate effect of making her sneeze. Again. And again. And…

When she finished her attempt at breaking a record, she opened tearing eyes to see a half-dozen hands holding out tissues.

"Um, thank you," she said as she plucked one. She dabbed at her nose one-handed since Hayder still hadn't relinquished his grip. Brave man considering she'd only barely missed his shoes during her latest spell.

"Hey, Hayder, whatcha doing holding hands with a wolf in cat territory?" At the shouted question, the hum in the room quelled.

Damn, she'd forgotten for a moment she was surrounded by shifters. Lionesses to be exact, the true hunters in any pride. Vicious felines she wouldn't stand a chance against, especially with her wolf in hiding.

"She better not pee in the halls. I hear their kind like to do that you know."

"No they don't," said a young girl with rainbow-streaked hair. "It's trees and fire hydrants you gotta watch out for."

A woman with a ring in her nose snorted. "You're all idiots. Those are the spots dogs mark. She's a wolf, and you're scaring the crap out of her." Blue eyes, set in a face creased with age, turned to face her. The woman spoke to her soothingly. "Don't worry about what they're saying. We're allies. You'll come to no harm among us."

"Unless you pee in the halls."

"Or eat the last piece of cake." Someone poked the chubby speaker in the side, and she whirled with a, "What? Just saying what we're all thinking."

"Forget thinking. It's obvious it hurts too much," yet another lioness muttered. "What I'd like to know, the smart questions here are, who is this girl, and what is she doing here?"

In a panic, Arabella peered up at her guard. Should she answer, and what should she say? Give the truth or spout a lie? Or would lying be worse? What if Hayder and his alpha had already established an identity for her? What—

Hayder saved her from answering. "Ladies—"

Snickers. "He called us ladies."

"—this is Arabella, Jeoff's sister. You all know Jeoff."

"Yeah, he's the hottie in the tight jeans who sings in that band."

"He sings?"

"Among other things."

The matronly one, who asked who Arabella was, sighed as she planted her hands on her hips. "Would you all shut up? Some of us are trying to get answers here. I sense something juicy, so zip it before I do something that requires you getting your jaw wired shut."

Funny how they all quieted, and yet none of them looked cowed at the threat. They were all, however, united in their curious stares aimed at her.

When Arabella would have tucked behind Hayder's back to make herself less of a visual target, he pulled her forward and stood her before him, one hand on each shoulder, anchoring her in place. "Jeoff asked the pride to lend its protection. Some assholes want to force Arabella here into marrying some dick so he can get his hands on her fortune. There's also talk of killing her once the paperwork is done. I don't think we should allow that."

As summaries went, it was accurate and succinct. What she didn't expect was the outrage and...support?

Forget the cowed women of her old pack. The females surrounding her all bore a challenging glint in their eye and boastful suggestions.

"Let them come and try to take her. We'll show them what women's lib is all about," one of them shouted.

"Woo hoo! A new fur coat and in time for winter," another hollered.

"Someone make sure we replaced the mop from the last time we had to show someone a lesson."

"Luna, we need to make an appointment to get our nails sharpened."

Arabella blinked, several times, but she somehow resisted the urge to jam a finger in her ear and wiggle. Why bother? It wasn't her ears that were defective. Either she'd finally snapped, or she surely dreamed. It was the only explanation for the insanity she'd encountered since her arrival.

More than likely, she'd fallen asleep in her old prison and dreamed everything from the rescue to the improbability surrounding her.

But what a dream. If only it were true. And if only she had an ounce of their courage so she could face her old pack and fight for her right to make her own choices.

Fighting hurts.

The faint whimper and reminder quelled any exhilaration she might have briefly felt. While their spirit and intentions were good, reality was another thing.

Apparently Hayder thought so, too, because he said, "Now, now, ladies. No starting any shit."

Hayder was right. Head down. Voice meek. Don't—

It seemed Hayder wasn't done. "I mean it. No starting trouble, but you can taunt. Taunt loud. Taunt mercilessly. Drive them to the brink and make them hit first. Then you can bring it. Just be sure to save a piece of those curs for me. I've got a few words my knuckles would like to say." He shook a fist as his utterly male announcement was met with cheers and fist pumps.

They're nuts. All of them. Or high on catnip.

Something was obviously whacky about their enthusiasm. Even her old pack never planned for mayhem with such glee.

It was to an excited hum—and talk of nail-filing methods—that Hayder once again dragged her, this time toward the glass doors at the front of the building.

She tried one last-ditch protest. "We shouldn't go out. We'll order in."

He halted. "You mean go back up to your condo where we'll be alone, just you, and me, and"—he purred—"chow down on takeout Chinese food while we watch Indiana Jones?"

She couldn't help but gape at him.

"Were you expecting me to say something else?"

"No. Of course not." She stammered the words and blushed hot because she had, indeed, imagined a different ending to his sentence.

"Never fear, baby. We will make good use of that king-sized bed I spotted in the bedroom, after we come back from dinner. First, though, I need to see your face when you eat that brownie and then compare that expression to the one you'll wear when I make you come the first time."

Only cats were always graceful. She stumbled, right into his arms.

Achoo!

Chapter Five

The speed at which his need to seduce Arabella came proved almost as fast as her sneezes every time she got near him.

A less vain man might have wanted something to soothe his bruised ego. Hayder merely took her allergy as a challenge.

We'll look into getting those shots. The kind the doctor gives for severe allergies. Or I'll invest in a tissue company. Hey, I bet Aunt Berna would make me some hankies.

What about fighting her allure instead?

Say what?

The oddball thought hit him out of nowhere as he walked on the sidewalk, Arabella tucked into his side. Exactly why was he looking for solutions? What happened to living his life as he was currently? Where did this insane urge to give in to fate come from?

Look at the facts. He barely knew Arabella, and yet he was ready to jump, with his whole body, into the whole mating ring. What the hell?

This lack of control had to stop. Hayder was his own man. He'd make his own choices when it came to whom he settled down with. Feeling attracted and sorry for the she-wolf at his side wasn't a good enough excuse to give up his lifestyle.

Especially since he'd probably quickly tire of her

once the novelty of seduction was gone.

Yet this is the first time I've ever wanted to seduce a woman so badly.

This was also the first time a woman made him want to protect. Who did that pack think they were, terrorizing the girl and trying to force her into an unwanted claiming?

No one claims what is ours.

Would you stop that? Hayder snapped back. It was certainties like the one his lion kept pushing that had Hayder all messed up. Even worse, by his actions and words, he was leading the girl on.

He couldn't in fairness seduce her knowing he had no intention of settling down any time soon.

That's what you think.

Lions perhaps couldn't chuckle, but his certainly tried. It made a guy want to go pet a mouse just to antagonize his feline side.

The walk to the restaurant didn't take long, but Hayder kept a close watch the entire way, from the circular driveway that led from the condo to the sidewalk on the street, to the shadowy alleys between buildings that could house any source of menace.

Alas, they made it to the restaurant unmolested. A shame. He did so enjoy a bit of sport before dinner.

Holding open the door to the restaurant, he finally let go of her hand, only so he could sweep his arm, gesturing for Arabella to enter.

It might have proven a lot more romantic had a minivan not chosen that moment to jump the curb and bump him in the hip, knocking him off balance. Then, the van, while still rolling, had its side door slide open. Arms emerged and snatched Arabella!

She squeaked, the panic in her eyes clear, the

pleading expression aimed his way utterly heart rending. He might have kept his human skin—barely—but he still roared.

"Get your hands off her!"

The dumbfucks didn't listen. The minivan bumped down off the curb, and the door slid shut, enclosing Arabella inside. The van gathered speed, but so did Hayder.

The van might have nudged him, but the forming bruise didn't bother him as he pounded the pavement in hot pursuit.

Lucky him, the traffic prevented the van from just speeding off. Dodging cars in a game of *Catter*—which in the online version involved water, cars, and dogs—he closed the gap. Before the van could shoot into the open and take off, Hayder bunched his legs and pushed.

He soared, arms extended Superman style, and caught the roof rail for the van. Fingers clamped the track, securing him. He held on tight as the van swerved, his whole body swinging, his legs a pendulum.

When his body swung back, he took a moment to pull himself inch by inch on the rails until he'd heaved his body onto the roof of the moving vehicle.

Dimly, he heard the surprised shouts of onlookers and the honks of cars as the van dipped and cut across lanes of traffic, a frantic zigzag meant to dislodge him.

Like hell. He wasn't going anywhere unless he had Arabella with him. Pulling himself even further forward, his hair streamed back from his head as the van finally found a clear spot and accelerated.

Muscles in his arms and shoulders bunched as he fought against the pull of the wind streaming over the roof. He stuck his head over the front edge and sported a ferocious upside-down grin as he surprised the driver of the vehicle and his passenger.

"Hello," he mouthed. "It's a fine day for a drive, don't you think?"

Apparently they didn't agree. They braked.

Good thing he'd expected it. His body flew forward, but he kept his grip on the rails, even if it wrenched his wrists.

His heavy body hit the hood of the van and left an impressive Hayder-sized dent. Since the van was stopped, probably not for long, Hayder didn't waste time. He let go with one hand and punched the windshield.

It hurt. He might have broken a knuckle or two, which would take a few days to heal, but it was so worth the look on the guy's face when Hayder reached through the fist-sized hole, grabbed him by the shirt, and yanked him forward, rapping his face off the glass. A few more tugs and smacks further shattered the glass. The abused windshield collapsed.

By this time, the driver was unconscious and no more fun to play with. However, his passenger, who'd spent a moment watching in stunned silence, now wanted to join in the fun.

"Want a turn? Give me just a second." Banging the driver one last time off the steering wheel, Hayder released him before reaching in for the passenger.

Hayder snagged him with two hands and hauled him out onto the hood, even as a third guy tried to wiggle through the front seats to help his buddy.

A grin split Hayder's lips. "You stay right there, my pudgy canine friend. I'll be right back for you."

First, though, Hayder stood and hauled his

newest opponent to his feet. He shook him. "Who are you, and what do you want with Arabella?"

When the wolf—distinguishable by his stink— didn't reply, Hayder head-butted him. His mother always did say he had a hard head, and he liked to put it to use.

"I asked you a question. Answer."

This time the dog didn't hold back. "I'm Davis from the Northern Lakes Pack."

"Arabella's old pack?"

He nodded.

"Are you and your buds the only ones hunting her?"

He hesitated.

Hayder held him off the hood of the van and shook him, violently, until the wolf's head whiplashed. "Answer me, you dumbfuck."

"I'll talk." The boy stunk of fear. Not so brave when confronted with a real predator. "We're not alone. The whole pack is here, plus some. Word has gotten out about her fortune and the challenge for alpha. There's a bounty for whoever brings her back before the full moon."

They'd placed a price on her head? Just how much money were they talking that these morons would risk so much to nab her?

Hayder dragged the boy close and made sure he had his full attention as he growled. "You tell your pack, and anyone else looking for her, that she's staying with the pride. She's ours now. And if you want her, you'll have to go through us. You can find us at the condo, company headquarters, and the restaurant most days. If no one is there to kick your ass, then stick around. I know a couple felines who are looking to line their closets with fur before winter."

With that invitation to tango, Hayder tossed the young wolf to the side. He had better things to do than waste his time with an unworthy opponent.

Such as chase down the assholes who thought they could drag his Arabella away.

It wasn't just his lion that liked to hunt down prey.

He didn't run, how undignified, especially when a firm stride would do. It wasn't hard to follow the trail. The scent of wolf proved thick, the untenable aroma of her fear an urge to move faster.

He couldn't spot them, and the minor foot traffic on the sidewalk was not enough to hide. They must have entered a building or alley. Rather than searching all of them, he let his nose do its job. Big breath in.

Filter the smells.

Aha.

There, up the sidewalk a few more storefronts then into an arcade. The wolves that dragged her probably hoped to hide their scent and sneak out the back. Except Hayder knew this place. He knew where the door to the alley was, thus, when the steel door swung open, he stood there, arms crossed waiting for them.

"Shit, he's here. Get back inside," the chubby one grunted.

"Oh, don't leave on my account. I insist you stay." And to make sure they did, he kicked the door shut.

The two thugs backed away from him, the one who needed to invest in a treadmill holding Arabella, who hung limp in his grasp, before him as a shield.

She was alive. However, her eyes bore a resigned expression Hayder didn't like at all. "Baby, are you all right? Did they hurt you?"

The answer was moot. At this point, he was going to punish them no matter what, violently. They'd done the unforgivable when they'd taken Arabella and scared her. However, if they'd actually hurt her, or if she cried…

We'll make them wish their mother had a headache the night they were conceived.

Rawr.

Her reply emerged so soft he almost missed it. "I told you this would happen. They'll never let me be free."

How utterly convinced she seemed and miserable. Totally unacceptable.

"Don't you dare take this without a fight," he growled.

The chubby one should have spent more time on expanding his mind instead of his waistline because he showed no sense at all when he said, "Bella here knows her place, and after the next full moon, it will be on her knees, serving the new alpha of the pack."

Hell no. Hayder didn't even think twice about it. His fist shot out, and it connected to the idiot's nose with a satisfying crunch, and that left one wolf. An even dumber wolf that seemed to think the switchblade he'd pulled out of a pocket and waved around would really make a difference.

"Are you stupid enough to think you can take me with that puny knife?" Hayder couldn't stem the incredulity in his query.

"Stay back, cat, or else. It's silver."

Silver, which meant painful if he got sliced with

it. Harder to heal, too. But a three-inch blade wasn't going to keep Hayder away from his woman.

As beta, though, he did try to give the idiot a chance. Show patience before acting, or so he'd been taught as part of those anger management courses Leo made him take. Hayder employed one of the tricks to control impulsive acts. He counted. "Three."

"I'll cut you." Slash. Slash. The knifeman sketched lines in the air.

"Two."

"I mean it."

"One. You're dead." Hayder took a step forward even as the last dumb wolf took a step back, one hand clamped around Arabella's arm.

Lightning fast, Hayder shot a hand out to grab the wrist of the guy wielding the knife. This fellow had slightly faster reflexes than his pack brothers and actually managed to score a line of red across his palm.

The blood didn't bother Hayder. 'Twas but a scratch.

However, the coppery scent did something to Arabella.

Up snapped her head. Her nostrils flared. Her brown eyes took on a wildness. Her lips pulled back in a snarl.

"Don't. Touch. Him!" With a screech, she turned on her captor and then proceeded to go rabid on his ass.

How cool.

Chapter Six

So not cool.

How dare Hayder ignore her wishes, not that she protested much aloud. True to habit, Arabella kept quiet as she sat tucked in the restaurant booth. Her only concession to her displeasure? A lower lip jutting in a pout.

The small moue of defiance had an audience since she didn't sit alone. Hayder lounged across from her on the bench. The maître d' had seated them in a booth that was much too large for the pair of them. It was private too.

Intimate as well with the flickering candle on the table that cocooned them in a pocket of warm light. Thinking of warm... The U-shaped leather seat proved chilly against her bottom and did nothing to temper her mood that wavered between bemused and sulking.

Bemused because, while she couldn't remember much of what happened, she did recall Hayder having to drag her off Jim, the pig who had once elucidated, in great detail, the disgusting things he'd do to her when she was his mate. But knowing Jim's intentions wasn't what turned her into an out-of-control wild woman. No, her temporary snap was all because of the smug lion across from her.

Jim had made Hayder bleed, nothing life

threatening as wounds went, and yet something in her snapped. *How dare Jim hurt him!* Odd how the injury to another precipitated her to action, and yet, when people offered her violence, she tucked her head and took it. *Why can't I stand up for myself?*

Perhaps her act today would prompt her to fight more.

I fought and won. Won, even if she had no idea how.

Hayder didn't seem to question the how. Once he'd dragged her away, screaming and threatening vile injury to Jim's manparts, Hayder swung her around with an exuberant whoop.

"You kicked ass, baby. I knew there was a wild woman hiding in there. And I'll bet you worked up an appetite."

She did hunger—Arabella wasn't a girl to skip meals—but the attempted kidnapping had made something very clear. It wasn't safe out in public, and she pointed that out. "I told you it was dangerous out here," she accused, still riding high on the exhilaration from the fight.

"I was there to protect you, and given I had to drag you off that guy, who I'm pretty sure will require a few stitches, you know how to defend yourself."

A first. She didn't know what had come over her. She smelled blood, Hayder's to be exact, and lost her freaking mind. Literally.

And I liked it.

But that one act was an aberration. She couldn't count on surprise and adrenaline to protect her again, and her old pack would try again, of that she was certain. "You should have just let them take me. They're never going to stop."

"Letting them take you isn't an option."

"Because of your promise to Jeoff."

"No, because I wouldn't let those pricks take anyone, especially given their intention to force a mating."

Why did his generic reply depress? "By protecting me, though, you're putting yourself in danger."

"Bah." He scoffed. "What danger?"

She blinked. "Did you bang your head? Or don't you recall what just happened? They ran into you with their van, kidnapped me off the street, then tried to kill you by flinging you off. Oh, and then they tried to knife you." She couldn't help but almost yell her reply, still in shock over his actions.

Again, a derisive noise escaped him. "Ha. You call that danger? I see it more as sport. And just so you know, even if they had managed to fling me off, they wouldn't have gotten far. The pride owns this town. You didn't seriously think I was the only one watching, did you? The hunters from the pride were shadowing us every step of the way."

"What hunters? I didn't see anyone."

"You weren't supposed to."

Leaving the unconscious wolves in the alley, he'd tucked her hand into the crook of his arm, ignored her hat trick of a sneeze, and dragged her out onto the sidewalk. Once there, he pointed and cheerfully announced, "There's Luna and Zena pretending to window shop. In that car over there, the bright red one with the blonde behind the wheel, that's Stacy. I'm pretty sure Melly is on the rooftop cursing me out for ruining her fun. She does so love to swoop in and kick some tail. Personally, I think she watched one too many

Batman movies as a child. At least she stopped wearing the damned leather suit the last time her lioness got tangled in it."

To the inane rendition of his pride's characteristics and embarrassing stunts, Hayder walked them a few blocks to the restaurant, A Lion's Pride, a steakhouse chain owned by none other than Hayder's alpha.

Despite her feeble protest they should go back to the condo—even more feeble once she smelled the heavenly aroma of charred meat wafting—he soon had her ushered into a booth and told the waiter to, "Get us some of your finest champagne. Arabella, here, just kicked some serious ass, and that is cause for celebration."

She just about groaned. Great, he wanted to celebrate an act that would probably come back to beat her when Jim and others from the pack caught up to her again.

What was I thinking? She knew better than to retaliate. Defiance hurt more in the end than the brief pleasure of fighting back.

Add to that Hayder's open taunt to attack and she harbored no doubt her old pack would come hunting for her again. They'd keep coming and coming until they got her back to the bosom of the pack. Then, they'd make her pay before she died.

"You've got that look again," Hayder announced as he snapped his fingers in front of her eyes.

"What look?" she mumbled as she stared at the polished wood grain of the table. No tablecloths adorned the surface, just pure wood that really couldn't hold her attention away from the man across from her.

"That look that says woe is me I've given up. It's not a good look."

"Why do you care?"

"Because."

"Because isn't an answer." The words left her mouth, and she didn't have time to be horrified by her rebuttal as his laughter washed over her.

"Well, that's a little better. You should let that spirit of yours out more often."

Arabella would love to let her out, but she was buried so deep she doubted she'd manage to coax her into daylight again.

Idly she traced her name on the surface of the table, something to stare at instead of him. "I don't understand you." She didn't. How dissimilar he was to the men she'd grown accustomed to. In some ways, he reminded her of her brother, Jeoff.

Except I never wanted to kiss my brother.

"But isn't the not understanding what makes me all the more intriguing? Just think, I'm like a mystery gift, baby, one you can unwrap anytime. Preferably with your lips and teeth."

Outrageous words, but her body was the one displaying the even more shocking reaction. The blatant flirtation caused a chain reaction. She could no more help the tightening of her nipples into hard points than she could hide the heat surely coloring her cheeks.

"I don't know how you can be so flippant." Or say such dirty things. *Say them again.*

"If I say 'because' again, will you get rough with me? I have a four-poster bed and plenty of neckties." He winked.

Rendered speechless, and all because she couldn't help a mental image of him spread-eagle on a bed, wearing much less clothing. Then again, why would he wear clothes when he could wear a naked Arabella?

Oh my.

Stop it.

Focus. Focus on something other than him. Ignore the hormones that, repressed for so long, burst in a tidal wave of awareness.

She had to snap out of it. Control herself. She couldn't go lusting after every hot guy she met now that Harry was gone. Her lonely body—with its cobwebbed memory of sensual pleasures—would have to wait until she was able to live out in the open, a mistress of her own choices. Mistress of her own body.

Even if his mastery of it would rock my world.

Sigh. There was no helping it.

Or ignoring him.

"I can see you're seriously thinking about it. Why not make it a reality? We could be at the condo in less than five minutes."

The determined glint in his eyes said it might even take only four minutes. Three if he really pushed it.

She was almost tempted to tell him she'd time him to see. Thankfully, common sense—also known as the chastity belt to her sex life—made her say, "I won't get involved with you."

"Is your answer because of your allergies? Because I'm willing to ignore them."

"My allergies are a good reason, but not the biggest one. Getting involved with me is too dangerous and—" Forget finishing that sentence.

Hayder moved too fast for her to stop him, especially considering he did the unexpected. He shut her up with a kiss!

A fist or a slap, even a kick, with those she'd

come to recognize the warning signs and knew how to brace against them. But Hayder showed no sign of his intentions, unless the intensity in his amber eyes meant something. Around the leather bench he slid, as if it were buttered, until he invaded her space and claimed her next word with his lips.

He silenced her with a kiss. A beautiful, soft, sexy, and sensual kiss. Even more astonishing than the heated pleasure of his touch, she did nothing to stop him.

More.

From the moment he plastered his lips to hers, she stopped thinking. There was only one thing that mattered. More. More of him. More of this.

In that moment, right and wrong ceased to exist. Danger and unsuitability, even allergies, took a back seat to the electric slide of his mouth, coaxing her lips apart, sucking on them until they throbbed.

With expert skill, he brought her senses alive, holding her in his arms while tugging at her bottom lip with his teeth.

It wasn't enough. *I want more.*

So did he. He dragged her onto his lap, or did she crawl onto it? Did it matter? It brought them closer. The heat of his body merging with her own. The irritating chafe and titillation of having body parts, still clothed, rubbing against each other.

How much nicer if those layers would disappear. Then they could press against one another, skin to skin.

Alas, for now, only their mouths joined and their breaths mingled. Soft sounds blended, and his essence surrounded her.

A presence intruded.

Grrrr.

The interruption was met with a menacing growl, a low rumble that shook the ribs.

Arabella whipped around and bared her teeth so fast it took her a moment to even realize it had happened. A menacing tightness to her eyes and her lip pulled back in a snarl, she eyed the interrupter.

The waiter, a tiger by the smell, didn't bat an eyelid. "Your champagne, ma'am."

"You can take your champagne and—" She almost said shove it into a place where the sun never shone.

Almost.

She shouldn't have thought it, let alone begun saying it.

A good thing she was already seated or she might have fallen over in astonishment. What was happening to her?

Why was she so mad at the waiter? So very, very mad.

She tried to stifle it as she stared blankly at the offered bottle and glasses.

Throw them at his head.

She knew that insidious whisper. But she didn't reply. She was too busy clenching her hands so as to not act.

Hayder planted a kiss on her neck. Through her whole body shiver, she heard him say, "Just put the stuff on the table, bud. And next time, don't sneak up on my baby here when she's busy. She might look sweet on the outside, but she's got a vicious core, and she will hurt you."

He said it teasingly, and she might have thought he mocked her, except a part of her agreed with his words. She wasn't pleased at all at the interruption, and she still wanted to snap at the waiter.

Even if I should be thanking him.

He'd interrupted a moment of madness. Now, with clarity returning, she could analyze what had happened and allow herself to be properly horrified.

She shouldn't be kissing Hayder in a public restaurant. Hell, she shouldn't be kissing him at all. She barely knew him. She was only a job for him. He didn't care for her. His only reason for being with her was for protection. And what about her allergies? What about them? She'd not sneezed once during their kiss. Maybe—

Achoo!

Nope. Not gone. While they might have remained quiescent for a moment while they kissed, they still lurked, ready to go off without notice. Further proof of why she should keep her distance.

However, Hayder apparently didn't know how to take a hint. The idiot cat didn't move. She aimed her next exhalation his way.

Take that, personal space invader.

"Done?" he asked with an arched brow.

"No, so you'd better move." *Achoo.*

"You know, baby, there are other ways of marking me with your scent."

Stubborn cat.

With another growl, this time an intentional one, she slid off his lap and wiggled around on the slippery seat, giving herself as much space as possible.

As if there was enough space in the world for her to ignore the charismatic man across from her.

He didn't seem perturbed at all by her scowl or the fact she'd soaked his shirt. He poured them both a drink.

She might have refused it except she needed something to cover the taste of him in her mouth. She grabbed the proffered glass stem and tilted the contents of the flute into her mouth.

The bubbly champagne tickled its way down, leaving in its wake a warm lassitude.

Dinner passed in silence, and the occasional groan as she ate. It was that good.

As for the dessert, it proved even better than he claimed.

The low, rumbling hum rolled from her mouth as the chocolate and caramel hit her tongue. "Oh my god that's good. So good. So incredibly delicious." She groaned that last bit.

"Holy fuck, baby. Stop that, or I won't be responsible for what I do."

She opened her eyes to find his smoldering gaze on her. The tension in his body practically vibrated the space in between them.

Say something. Tell him to stop staring at you. To stop looking like he'll devour you.

But I like it. She wanted his ardent flirtation. But she also wanted control. How to achieve it? The solution seemed too simple.

Fight sensuality with…sensuality.

"Stop what?" she innocently said.

Holding his stare, she brought a heaping forkful of nirvana to her mouth. She slid the top of the spoon between her lips, lapped it with the tip of her tongue.

A nerve twitched in his cheek.

The spoon pushed its way into her mouth. She sucked the sugary bite from it.

He swallowed.

Slowly, she withdrew the spoon and licked it

clean.

He groaned. "That has got to be the cruelest thing anyone has ever done to me."

She could have giggled at his woebegone expression except someone big, blonde, and wanting-to-die flounced up and practically threw herself at Hayder.

Grrr.

For a wolf who wouldn't come out of hiding, someone was acting pretty dominant.

No, she's jealous.

It was the green-eyed monster making her agitated and with good reason, given the giant hussy hugged Hayder and smooched him on both cheeks. It took a lot of will to not dive across the table and claw out her eyes. Instead, Arabella's nails dug crescents into her palms.

"Cousin. It's been so long," the hussy gushed.

Cousin?

"If you ask me, it hasn't been long enough," he replied. "What trouble has brought you out this way, Meena?"

"Did you know it's been over ten years since I visited Arik's pride?"

"Let's make it twenty before the next."

If Arabella expected Hayder's odd cousin Meena to take offense, she was wrong. The big blonde giggled. "Oh, Hayder. You know you love me."

"Like I love a tick. I still haven't forgiven you for that stunt you pulled on me."

"That was years ago, and I see your eyebrows grew back."

With a growl, Hayder dumped his cousin off his lap and slid away. But Arabella did notice that, however much he grumbled, he was gentle in his manhandling.

Arabella did not prove so gentle when Meena made a stab at her cake. *Mine.*

Before Arabella could blink, she'd slapped the blonde girl's hand and sent her fork flying.

They both gaped at each other.

"I guess you're not into sharing," Meena stated.

Nope. Not her dessert, or her man.

He's not my man.

Whatever.

Again, Meena didn't take offense, not judging by her wide smile. "Feisty. Awesome. I like her, coz. You should keep her."

"No." Arabella spoke instantly.

So did Hayder. "Yes."

His answer was the complete opposite of hers, and stunning.

For a moment nothing was said.

Meena swung her head one way then the other, obviously noting the relationship tennis match going on. "Damn. Looks like I got here in time to catch some drama. When are you going to admit your undying love and passion for each other?"

"Never."

"Later.

Again with the polar-opposite answers. Arabella tired of the game. Ignoring them both, she slid from the booth and stood. "I'm going back to the condo. I'm tired."

"I'll go with you."

"Don't bother. I don't need you." Such a lie.

"And since you don't need this cake, mind if I finish it?" Without waiting, Meena snared the edge of the plate and dragged it to her.

Arabella almost snatched it back. *My precious*

yummy.

Instead, she spun on her heel and stalked away. The prickle between her shoulder blades let her know she wasn't alone.

"You do know I can't let you leave unaccompanied."

"What about the check?" she tossed over her shoulder. "Or are you going to dine and dash? Oh, sir." She waved at the maître d'. "He's trying to leave without paying." Her sudden temerity should have made him roar in rage—and she should have started running to avoid his revenge.

But clumsiness took her grace, and she stumbled as he chuckled. "Put it on my tab."

Wouldn't that just figure?

Angry, but why she couldn't have truly articulated, Arabella stepped from the noisy elegance of the restaurant onto the sidewalk. It still surprised her that they'd managed to avoid having the police called in over the hit and run by the kidnappers' van. Apparently, the pride owned the city in more ways than one.

Her sneakered feet didn't make much sound on the pavement, and Hayder made even less. With the wind blowing in the wrong direction, she didn't expect the arm that snaked around her waist.

She screamed and stiffened.

Hayder drew her in close, and she craned to peek up at him, caught a whiff, and sneezed.

Chapter Seven

Achoo.

Hayder resisted the urge to wipe his face. He knew she'd soaked him intentionally. She thought to provoke him. Tried to get him to react.

She is testing me.

And he intended to pass with flying colors.

So he let her get her little jab in. He let her spray him using her allergies as an excuse to keep him at bay. Now wasn't the time to push her. On the street, where he needed to remain alert, wasn't the place to discuss their impending future. A future together.

Burn the black book, disappoint the hundreds of women who'd never gotten to enjoy him, Hayder was officially off the market. He'd succumbed to the mating fever. It apparently had a lot in common with catnip. Irresistible and addictive.

Now if only he could get Arabella to feel it too. He'd caught a glimpse of her passion for him in the restaurant. Now to make her admit it and stop fighting it.

Once they reached the relative safety of the condo, and the heavy door shut behind them, he pounced. "So tell me, baby, why do you insist on pushing me away?" He tackled the question head-on.

"What makes you think I am?" She evaded the

question as she sank into the armchair, effectively placing herself out of reach. Or so she thought.

He didn't reply to her sidestepping query. Why bother when he could prove the truth of his statement. He scooped her from the chair, plopped down, and then tucked her onto his lap.

She bounced off it quicker than a bunny on its third cup of cappuccino.

"That's what I mean. Why won't you let me touch you?"

"You seriously have to ask?"

"I could ask while laughing, but I don't think it's funny. I want you to want me. I think you want to as well. And yet you're fighting it? Why?"

"Because I've known you only a few hours."

"Haven't you heard of love at first sight? Or we can call it the mating fever. Whatever the name, you know something is happening between us."

"It can't."

"Why?"

"Because I'm still technically in mourning."

"For a man who didn't treat you right."

"I never said that."

"I'm not a blind idiot, baby. Someone hurt you. Someone close. And while it pains me to admit it, I don't think Jeoff is the type of guy to cause that type of pain. Which means it was someone else close to you. Like your mate."

"You shouldn't speak ill of the dead."

"Or what? He'll come back to haunt me? I'd like that so I could teach the prick a lesson about being an asshole to a lady. He hurt you. He doesn't deserve any respect. I just wish I could have saved you from him sooner." Apparently something he said struck a chord because tears threatened to spill from her eyes. "Baby, don't cry. Why are you crying?"

"I'm not," she sniffled.

"You don't actually miss the prick who abused you, do you?" The very idea appalled him, and yet why else would she cry?

"Oh god, I don't miss him. At all. It's just…" She stopped.

Hayder told his kitty and his impatience to sit in a corner and wait. Give her a chance.

A tremulous breath wobbled from her. "You know, my brother would have taken care of Harry if given a chance. But he would have done it because he had to. I'm family."

"I'm not, and I'll tell you right now, had I come across that prick abusing you, I would have killed him." Laws or not. Abuse should never be tolerated.

She blinked rapidly, failing in her battle against the tears. Her voice trembled. "And that's just it. You really would fight for me. You already did, earlier today. You could have let them take me and washed your hands clean. Yet you didn't. You came to my rescue, and the weird part is, I think you'd do it again."

"As many times as it takes to keep you safe. I know it's crazy, and we haven't known each other long, but there's something happening between you and me, baby. Something crazy. Wild. Meant to be. Don't tell me you don't feel it too?"

"I do." How soft the admission. How fearful the truth. "And it scares me. You scare me. What if I'm wrong?"

It was that genuine terror that let him say, "You're not, but I won't push." Not tonight at least. He'd give her a little space to come to terms with what was happening. "Go to bed. Alone." Oh, how he wanted to yowl mournfully. "If you need me, I'll be here or not far. You don't have to worry anymore. I won't let you come to harm."

He'd guard her with his life.

As if fearful he'd change his mind, Arabella fled without another word—or even a good-night kiss—the click of the lock a scraping wince to his pride.

What happened to her that she was so scared to trust? How dare her mate and pack break her so thoroughly? And broken her they had.

During the course of the day, he'd seen the glimpses of another Arabella, a brave one. How much had this Harry, so-called pack alpha, and the others hurt her to quell such a fiery side?

Watching that bedroom door close—separating them—proved harder than he would have expected. Only a few hours since he'd met Arabella and already his life had changed. His whole mental state had.

For the first time he could understand why people claimed love at first sight. In his case, it might have been scent, but it didn't change the fact that he was falling fast and hard for the timid she-wolf. While her skittish side brought out the protector in him, he loved the hints of the fighter in her, the spirit that struggled to free itself.

He wanted to help her unleash that inner courage and feistiness he suspected lurked. It would happen, once he got her to rid herself of that awful fear.

A fear some assholes seemed determined to perpetrate.

Hayder didn't bother checking the time when he left the condo. He banged on the closest door and waited with arms crossed, foot tapping. It opened a moment later on a tousled-hair Luna, who scowled.

"What do you want?"

"A lifetime supply of porterhouse steaks in my freezer." Like duh. What feline wouldn't?

"Smartass."

"Thank you. I knew those IQ tests I took in college were wrong. But enough of my mental greatness, I need a favor."

"I am not lending you my eighties greatest hits CDs again to use for skeet practice," she grumbled.

"That's not a favor. That's just making the world a better place. No, I need you to watch Arabella's place while I talk to the boss about her situation."

Obviously the rumor mill had been busy because Luna didn't question what he meant. "You really think those wolves would be stupid enough to try something here?" Luna slapped her forehead. "Duh. Of course they are. Must be something in their processed dog food that inhibits their brain processes."

"One, while I agree that pack is mentally defective, you might want to refrain from calling them dogs or bitches or any other nasty names in the near future."

"Why? Aren't you the one who coined the phrase 'ass-licking, eau de toilette fleabags'?"

Ah yes, one of his brighter inspirations after a few too many shots of tequila. "Yeah. But that was in the past. If I'm going to be mated to a wolf—"

"Whoa there, big guy. Back up. Mated? As in"— Luna hummed the wedding march—"dum-dum-dum-dum."

Hayder fought not to wince. Knowing he'd found the one and admitting it in such final terms were two different things. "Yes, mated. To Arabella."

"The girl who is allergic to you?" Luna needed the wall to hold her up as she laughed. And laughed. Then cried as she laughed.

Irritated, Hayder tapped a foot and frowned. It just made her laugh all the harder.

"It isn't that funny."

"Says you." Luna snorted, wiping a hand across her eyes to swipe the tears. "Oh, wait until the girls hear this."

"Could we hold off on that? It might help if I got Arabella to agree first." Which, given her past and state of mind, wasn't a sure thing.

"You're killing me here, Hayder. This is big news. Real big."

"I'll let you borrow my treadmill." Damned thing was nothing more than a clothes rack in his room. Indoor running just couldn't beat the fresh adrenaline of an outdoor sprint.

"Really big news," she emphasized.

He sighed. "Fine. You can borrow my car. But don't you dare leave any fast food wrappers in it like last time."

"Who, me?" The innocent bat of her lashes didn't fool him one bit.

Despite her playful demeanor, Hayder felt confident enough in her abilities as a fighter to leave her in charge of guarding his woman, a woman who snapped when he got hurt. It was enough to make a grown lion smile. But the locked door of his alpha's penthouse suite made him roar.

"Arik, damn you, I know you're in there. Open up."

"Doesn't anyone know how to use a fucking phone?" was the yelled reply.

Oh yeah, that stupid electronic device that he lost so often. Hayder kept a box of them in his place, along with some pre-paid phone cards so he could rapidly activate another each time he destroyed one.

"Fine. You want me to call. Ring! Ring! I need to come in and talk to you."

With a loud sigh that Hayder heard through the closed door, Arik, mumbling about pesky betas that didn't know their place and needed an ass whooping, opened the door.

It didn't surprise Hayder to see Arik clad in only track pants. Since the man had gotten mated to that hairdresser a little while back, he spent most of his evenings in private. Wagers were being placed on how long before that 'privacy' took fruit in his new human mate.

"What do you want that couldn't wait until the morning?" Arik asked as he led the way inside. The Pride's king headed to the bar he'd had installed in the corner of his living room. He pulled a bottle of whiskey from a shelf. He poured them each a generous dollop.

"I want permission to go after the Northern Lakes Pack."

"Am I going to regret asking why?"

"They're threatening Arabella."

"Who's that?"

"Jeoff's sister."

Arik tossed back the fiery liquid before asking with a frown, "Why the fuck would I let you start a war over Jeoff's sister?"

"Because those pricks attacked us on home turf."

A snort escape Arik. "Ah yes, that puny attempt at a kidnapping. You caused quite a stir with your antics.

Part of your stunt even made it onto *YouTube* before we could squash it. I had to have our PR department spin a Twitter thread on how it was part of a scene being taped for a movie."

"You can't blame me for that. I had to stop them." He did, but what he didn't tell Arik was he'd never once thought of the repercussions of his actions. He saw Arabella in danger and had to go to her rescue. Bystanders and witnesses be damned.

"I can see why you'd feel like you had to act. I mean, they made you look silly by catching you off guard like that, but, next time, could you be a little more discreet?"

"No." Why lie?

The reply took his leader aback. "What do you mean no? Discretion is a fact of life. One girl isn't worth drawing undue attention to ourselves."

"One girl might not be, but my mate is."

Want to stop conversation dead? Drop a bombshell.

"Close your mouth, Arik, before you catch flies." Only Arik's mate could hope to tease him like that and get away with it. Dressed in yoga pants and a sweatshirt, Kira emerged from the bedroom and perched on a barstool.

"Did you hear what he said?" a still astonished Arik demanded.

"Yes. He's fallen victim to the love bug. I think it's cute."

"I would have said impossible," Arik muttered.

"You and me both, old friend. But, the fact of the matter is, I'm like ninety-nine percent sure that Arabella is supposed to be mine."

"And the one percent that isn't sure?"

"Is going to get eaten by my lion."

Kira snickered. "Someone's got it bad. And I'm not talking about your ragged split ends."

Affronted, Hayder slapped a hand to his precious mane. "Take that back. I do not have split ends."

"Come see me at the barbershop, and you won't. I'll get you fixed up." She made snipping sounds as she scissored her fingers then laughed at his wince.

"She's evil, Arik."

"And all mine," his alpha said with evident pride.

"So about that war on the Northern Lakes Pack?"

"As leader, I can't outright condone starting shit, but I'm also not going to stop you from taking care of unwanted visitors to our city. I hear the dog population has gotten out of control and could use some culling."

Oh he'd cull all right. Hayder would wipe any threats to Arabella clean. And enjoy it.

Rawr.

Chapter Eight

A cool breeze ruffled her fur as she tore through the shrouded forest.

Free. Free. Soon she'd be free.

Enough was enough. If her human half couldn't do what had to be done, then the wolf would.

No more of this hiding. No more of this shame.

Far, far away she'd flee and start over. A new and fresh start. If she could escape.

A baying rose behind her. *Awoo! Awoo!* It sounded natural, the howl of wolves also out for a nightly run. However, she could decipher the intent even if the ululations had no words

We're coming to get you. We're coming to hurt you. Run, run as fast as you can, you still can't escape the might of the pack.

Dammit. They'd discovered her gone and now chased after. Never mind her head start. Those that hunted were much larger and faster. If she still wanted to escape, then she needed to put more distance between them.

Faster she ran, her fours paws working in cadence, the calloused pads gripping at the ground, finding purchase on rocks and allowing her to nimbly leap over the fallen trunks that crossed her path.

A yip came from her left. A startling sound echoed as well to her right. Double damn. The hunters had flanked her.

Perhaps if she went one way, she could surprise the chaser and break free of the noose they drew tight.

She veered, aiming to the northeast, angling across, wondering if perhaps she'd get lucky and avoid the hunters altogether.

Breath in. Breath out. Hot steam that misted the air. The pants of exertion almost covered that of her path, the soft crunch of foliage and fallen leaves gunshot-loud in the still forest. All the little creatures were abed, or hiding. They knew better than to remain in the open when the hunt was on.

A solid weight slammed into her without warning. Down she crashed, the air knocked from her, leaving her without breath to even yelp. Pinned beneath a shaggy shape, she flailed, looking for purchase and a way to fling off her attacker. She craned her head, jaw snapping at the one who held her down.

But she was no match for the brute strength of the beast pinning her, a wolf she knew well. Too well to her dismay. Her mate.

My jailor.

The male who made her life a living hell. She wouldn't go back to him. She couldn't.

Rage filled her, an ire born of abuse and taunts that gave fuel to her adrenaline, strength to her muscles.

She fought, using every savage trick she knew, plus some she invented on the spot. Her small and tricky shape kept wiggling out of his grasp, but she couldn't quite flee as he pounced on her. Her sharp teeth were busy, clamping tight when she found flesh. She hurt him.

She. Hurt. Him. The exhilaration of knowing she could almost made up for the abuse she took in return.

Wet warmth along her ribs signaled an injury, and when she tried to put weight on her hind leg, agonizing pain shot through her. But she didn't give up. Actually she found a spurt of energy when she noted her mate tired. Size was well and good, but he lacked the stamina to maintain any kind of assault.

But, of course, the leader of her pack didn't work alone.

Just as she scrabbled free, leaving him panting and snarling, blood dripping into his eye from a gash on his head, his enforcers arrived. She didn't need to see the evil glare in their eyes or hear their vicious snarl to know she was in trouble. She knew these wolves. Knew them as men too. And what she knew wasn't good.

Their names didn't matter. What did was their intent. Their intent to harm.

They didn't care that she was smaller or female. They tore into her, taking down her tired frame and biting. Not gnashing hard enough to kill or to permanently injure, just enough to hurt. To bleed.

Relentless. Cruel. The agony made her gasp, and they wouldn't stop. As for her mate, he'd shifted and stood watching, his dark eyes glinting with triumph.

He noted her eyeing him. His smirk deepened. "Had enough yet? Tell your bitch to go away. I want to speak with my *wife*."

The wolf wanted to deny his demand. But she'd lost. More than lost, she'd caused so much harm to them.

The woman inside the wolf struggled to break free. Fur receded, and skin appeared, blood-streaked and mottled. Her mate's enforcers stood back, allowing her to shift.

On the ground, naked and hurt, Arabella panted, staring at the toes of her husband. Tears burned her eyes. "I didn't mean to run. Please. I'm sorry. I won't do it again." The words almost choked her, and they shamed her inner wolf.

The words did not help her case.

"You're right. You won't do it again because, this time, I'll teach you a lesson you won't forget. Boys. You know what to do."

Indeed they did.

Arabella curled into a ball and tried to shut her mind to the abuse that rained upon her. Her wolf whined to get out, but Arabella wouldn't let her free, wanting to protect her inner beast. The wolf tried to not hear Arabella's pleas for mercy. She whimpered at the shrill screams and despair. Nothing could stem the pain, a pain caused by choosing to run. *I did this. I did this to us.*

Arabella's wolf curled into a corner of Arabella's mind. Curled up, put her face in the fur of her tail. She hid, knowing that her defiance had led to this.

Stop. Please stop. No more. Please.

The memories of the blows faded, replaced by the soothing stroke of a gentle hand and soft words. "Wake up, baby. You're having a nightmare."

Arabella stilled mid whimper. Her body shivered in recollection, the skin clammy and cold. She wanted Hayder to go away. She didn't want him to see her like this. She didn't want anyone to see her like this.

Perhaps if she held still, he'd leave, leave her to the shameful memories of her failure.

As if Hayder would do such a thing. Instead, he pulled back the covers and crawled into bed with her.

Naked!

Forget feigning slumber. "What are you doing?"

she squeaked, flinching away from the heated skin that met hers. Not expecting a visitor, she'd gone to bed in a T-shirt and panties, adequate sleep time attire if it hadn't ridden up during her nightmare and if a very naked man hadn't thought to invade her space.

"I'm cuddling," he announced, not letting her escape. His arm snaked around her and drew her back into the scorching warmth of his body.

Much as she enjoyed it, she knew she couldn't allow it. "Where are your clothes?"

"In the other room."

"But why?" she sputtered.

"Oh come on, baby. Because I can't sleep in them of course."

"You were sleeping in the other room?" Where? The couch certainly wasn't long enough for his tall frame.

"Well duh. How else am I supposed to guard you?"

Of course he'd only remained out of duty, but it didn't explain his presence in her bedroom. "How did you get in here? I know I locked the bedroom door."

"Yeah, about that, I can't believe you locked me out!" He seemed more than a little offended.

The cracked doorjamb showed that hadn't proven much of an obstacle. "That didn't stop you I see."

"Only because I heard you crying. Bad dreams?"

Understatement. "You could say."

"Do you get them often?"

"Only since I escaped." Apparently, a fear of capture led to her reliving her last failed escape.

"Poor baby." He rumbled as he rubbed his cheek against her hair.

To Arabella's surprise, she didn't sneeze. Probably because of the triple antihistamine dose she'd taken before bed.

"I'm all right now. You can leave." Before she did something foolish that she would regret, like rub back.

He hugged her closer. "I'm not going anywhere."

"But…" What she meant to say got lost and forgotten as his lips brushed her nape.

A full-body shiver rocked her.

"But what, baby?"

What indeed? She tried to focus her thoughts. This was wrong—even if it felt right. "You shouldn't be here." He shouldn't be here naked and tempting her to do things she needed to abstain from. Things like wiggling her bottom closer to him, closer to the hard press of his arousal that triggered an answering wet heat in her sex. Things like turning around to face him so she could kiss him and recapture the insane passion of before.

So many things she wanted to do. So many reasons not to. "I'm fine now. You can return to the couch or floor or wherever you were sleeping." Naked. She really needed to stop obsessing about that.

"No."

"What do you mean no?" It only belatedly occurred to her that she wasn't acting meek or placating him. She was questioning and demanding. And he wasn't yelling or hitting. Instead, he was…nuzzling.

"No, as in I won't leave you not now, probably not ever. You know, you're really cuddly." He squeezed her. "And you smell delicious." He nosed her hair, his warm breath in and out provoking a shiver, the kind that shook her whole body and ended between her legs.

She tried to make sense of his words, even as he sought to steal all rational thought from her with his soft caresses. She managed to mutter, "I'm not ready for this. For you. It's too soon. Too much." Hayder overwhelmed her with not just arousal. He seemed to promise a future, one that, if real, she wanted. He offered her protection, the kind that would keep the pain away. He also encouraged her to be herself, to stand up for herself.

And part of standing up for herself was not letting him dictate—even if his dick proved tempting—when and how he'd get to sleep in her bed, with her.

She thought of giving him another warning. But no, she'd asked him twice. He'd refused to listen. He'd also told her to trust him.

Dared she test him?

Better now than later.

Before she changed her mind, she rolled in his arms. Lashes fluttered as she let her gaze meet his, the faint illumination from the night light in the bathroom letting her see his expression—a nightlight because she couldn't bear the dark.

She let her hands rest on the slightly furry chest. Breathing halted at the electric feel of his taut flesh under her fingertips.

Perhaps I'm being hasty. Maybe having him in bed isn't a bad thing?

His lips drew close as he whispered, "Oh, baby. I knew you'd come around."

He did, did he? That only strengthened her resolve. She murmured back, "I said no."

And then she shoved.

Chapter Nine

She shoved me out of the bed!

The realization hit him as hard as the floor. His feline grace failed him. Far from hanging its head in shame, his inner lion rolled in mirth, tufted tail practically wagging.

Not funny.

Except it was. He had a feeling this more assertive side of Arabella was his fault. Since the moment they'd met, he'd encouraged her to not take any shit, and apparently she'd decided to start with him.

Dammit. When he'd told her to not let the world stomp all over her, he should have specified his exemption. *I'm her mate. Isn't there a rule that says she can't kick me out of bed?*

Except she'd yet to realize what he had. Was it only a day ago since his life changed? Not even.

At this rate, he'd be picking out fucking China patterns by noon.

Completely emasculated and by a woman who wanted nothing to do with him.

Flipping to his knees, he sat up and rested his chin on the mattress. Arabella faced him, eyes wary, breathing shallow as she waited for his reaction.

More like she waited to see if he'd explode. She'd learn. Hayder would never harm her, but he would use his infamous kitty-cat eyes against her.

He stared. *You know you want me. You know you need me. Come on, baby. Melt. Melt for your lion.*

She stared right back.

Hmm, this wasn't working as planned.

He let the left side of his lip curl into a grin, tugging his cheek and popping his infamous dimple.

"I know what you're doing."

"What?"

"Trying to manipulate me into letting you back into bed."

"Is it working?"

For a moment her expression shifted, a quick flip of emotions as she struggled to answer. "Yes it's working. But I wish it wasn't."

"Why? Why fight it?"

"Because I think I need time."

It turned out there was something more powerful than his dimple. Her honesty.

He groaned. "I think you were sent to kill me. Fine. If you insist, I'll respect you even if I'd rather debauch you."

Her eyes widened.

"Respect doesn't mean I'm going to lie, baby. I want you. Bad. But I'll listen to what you want. For now." And, yes, he said it ominously. Let her think about it. Think about him. Soon even she wouldn't be able to deny they were meant for each other.

He stood, all six foot plus naked feet of him. And, yes, that did put a certain part of his anatomy in perfect view of a certain shocked gaze.

A sucked-in breath, cheeks that darkened, a certain awareness sizzling between them. She couldn't hope to hide her pleasure or interest in what she saw.

"Sweet dreams, baby." He winked and then turned, resisting an urge to catch her staring at his ass. He knew she was. He could feel the crazy heat as she traced his path out of the room.

Go back. Want to snuggle.

His lion couldn't understand why they were back in the living room with its cramped couch that wouldn't allow him to stretch out. Why couldn't they snuggle in the nice warm bed and, even better, cuddle with a nice warm mate?

Respect, my furry friend.

A lion had no use for respect though. His worldview was much simpler. Ours. Bed. Hungry. Not hungry for a steak but, rather, a sweet, creamy pie.

Hayder groaned. No need to keep reminding him of what he was missing. He knew. He hated it, but her wants had to take precedence over his. Argh.

How the hell was he supposed to go back to sleep now? As he lay on the couch, legs hanging over the armrest, his dick jutting, he couldn't help but wish he had a few lesser morals right now.

Time ticked, and he didn't sleep. He strained for any signs Arabella needed him. The nightmare didn't come back, and her sleep proved a lot smoother this second time round. Before, even with the door closed, he could hear her restless stirring.

When her tossing and turning became whimpers and cries and incoherent words that tore at him, he couldn't help himself.

He'd kicked in that door and gone to her.

What haunted her dreams? What frightened her so terribly? Whatever it was, he wanted to kill it, to tear the awful nightmare from her and completely obliterate it.

At around six a.m., he gave up on trying to go back to sleep. He called Leo, whose first reply instead of good morning or hello was, "Haven't you gone to bed yet?"

"Actually, I am just getting up."

That silenced Leo for a moment. "Are you sick?"

"No."

"You do realize it's not even close to noon, right?"

"I know what time it is," Hayder snapped, getting irked. "It's time for you to stop messing with me and bring me some clothes."

"Why would I do that? Where are you? Wait, don't tell me you stayed with the girl last night."

"She's mine. Where else would I be?"

"Dude, you met her yesterday."

"Yeah, and?"

"You. Met. Her. Yesterday." Leo enunciated each word slowly.

"I. Know," Hayder mocked. "What is this hang-up everyone has with time? She keeps saying the same thing. Who cares? She's the one."

"This is my fault," Leo grumbled.

"How do you figure that? Are you in charge of the fates and the decision on who belongs together?"

"No, but I might have knocked some sense into you one too many times."

"Aren't you just the comedian? But this is no joke. Arabella's mine, and that's that. Now would you bring me some clothes?"

"What about Jeoff?"

"What about Jeoff?"

"You don't think her brother might have an

issue with you hooking up with his sister, who, by all accounts, is vulnerable right now."

"Hey, are you implying my Arabella has loose morals? I'll have you know she turned me down. Would you believe she shoved me out of bed? Told me to go away?" Incredulity still filled him.

It didn't take super hearing to catch Leo's snort of mirth. "Ha. In that case, maybe she is the one. You need a woman who can say no to you sometimes."

"You are not a nice omega, Leo."

"Nice is for pussies. Now, are you done whining, or should I come over there and really give you something to whine about?"

Hayder rubbed his jaw. "No need."

"Are you sure? You know I'm always ready to help a pride member in need."

"All I need right now are some clothes."

"Give me a few minutes to wake up, and I'll bring you some stuff."

"No need to rush. I'm going to have a shower first."

A shower and maybe a tug.

A man had needs after all.

A need that didn't diminish even after he stroked himself to climax, her name on his lips.

Damn.

Hopefully she wouldn't make him wait too long.

Chapter Ten

How long will Hayder agree to wait while I make up my mind?

The question followed her into sleep and was with her when she woke. Alone.

She should have celebrated the fact he respected her.

What a jerk.

This was one time she might not have minded a seduction, and that was what it would have been, seduction. Mutual desire erupting into volcanic pleasure.

How lovely.

Except it didn't happen because the jerk had listened to her wishes. Hayder went away—every naked and yummy inch of him.

We should have made him ours.

The stray thought didn't get analyzed, as a noise drew her attention. Heart pounding, she rolled to her side, only to freeze.

Gape.

She probably drooled a little, but she definitely didn't blink. She didn't dare close her eyes because the mirage might disappear.

In the doorway to the bathroom stood a half-naked Hayder. A gleaming, skin moist, wearing only a small towel clutched around his loins Hayder. Lightly tanned flesh and muscles with their own muscles delineated every inch of his body.

He was every woman's fantasy, a walking temptation. A man who could have anyone he wanted, and yet, he appeared to want her. The proof was right there in the impressive tent at the front of his towel.

"Good morning, baby." He practically purred the words as he approached, loose hipped and captivating.

She couldn't swallow, let alone speak.

He crouched down, bringing himself eye level. "Cat got your tongue?" His eyes crinkled with mirth. "I don't have it yet, but I plan to later. Hungry?"

Yes. So hungry. She would love a nibble on that succulent lower lip of his. Would totally go for a suck of his tongue. Or maybe a suck of something more substantial.

"Baby, when you look at me like that…" Hayder blew out a breath. "Damn, but you've got me all worked up. I don't suppose you've changed your mind? It's still early. Scooch over a little, and I'll climb in with you. Then I can really show you a good morning."

She opened her mouth. Why was she stalling? What was she afraid of? She already knew she'd find great pleasure in his touch. How could a moment of decadence hurt?

"Y—"

Bang. Bang. Bang. "Arabella, it's me. Open up."

Forget what she'd been about to say. The arrival of her brother tossed a bucket of cold water on her.

"Are you fucking kidding me? I was this close," Hayder muttered as he got to his feet and left the bedroom, still only wearing a teeny, tiny towel to greet her brother.

Eep!

Arabella scrambled off the bed, but she wasn't quick enough getting out of the bedroom. She was in time, however, to hear, "Why you dirty fucking tom cat. How dare you seduce my sister!"

Smack.

Thump.

Rawr.

Grrr.

She leaned against the doorjamb as she watched Hayder, who'd lost his towel, and her brother, who wore a mighty scowl, rolling about on the floor in a flurry of fists and thrashing legs.

A rustle of movement drew her attention to the open condo door. A tousled blonde head peered in. "Everything okay?"

"I think so."

Amber eyes followed the destructive path of the combatants. "Men. Can't train them to behave inside and can't teach them to not piss on the furniture."

Arabella's mouth rounded in an O of surprise. Surely she'd misheard. "Pee?"

"Only my ex-boyfriend ever actually did that. He's the reason why I moved. Fucker would get drunk, break in through the window by the fire escape, and pee on my stuff. I'd get mad. He'd apologize. We'd have wild jungle sex, and then I'd kick him out and tell him to never talk to me again."

Still couldn't fathom the logic. "You had sex with a guy who peed on your couch?"

"Less the couch, more like the kitchen chair, so nothing I couldn't wipe up. And the worst part is the bastard would wait for me to wake up. I'd wander into the kitchen all oblivious like, totally in the buff, usually to find him munching one of my homemade cookies." The crazy blonde's brows shot up in an Aha moment. "Hey, wait a second. I wonder if that's why he got wasted so often?"

She'd just clued in. "He was after no-strings sex."

"I was actually talking about the cookies, but I think your explanation is more plausible."

Unlike this conversation. Arabella wondered if she'd somehow gotten transported to an alternate dimension. Where else would she converse about peeing ex-boyfriends while dressed in nothing more than a T-shirt and underwear while Hayder and Jeoff exchanged blows? Although those were less punches now and more a grunting struggle as they tired.

"I'm Luna by the way," the blonde in her doorway said with a wave and a bright smile.

"And I'm Arabella."

"I know who you are. Everyone does. The whole tower is abuzz about you and why you're here."

"I'm here because of the danger I'm in from my old pack. A danger that has apparently followed me here. Sorry about that." The people Arabella had met so far seemed rather nice, and she hated she'd brought her violent baggage and disturbed them.

Luna's freckled nose wrinkled. "What are you apologizing for? We're all excited about the chance to whoop some wolf butt. I was talking about the other thing we're buzzing about."

"What other thing?"

Luna rolled her eyes. "You know. *The thing.* You. Him." Luna made a squeaky noise as she poked a finger through a ring she made with her other hand.

Arabella's eyes widened. Was she implying…? "Oh no. We haven't— That is we're not— He's just here to protect me."

"Protect you from what, the clothing police?" Luna shot a pointed glance at Hayder, who currently sat on top of the struggle, bare ass exposed for anyone to see.

Grrrr.

Arabella didn't even notice she'd stepped in front of Luna, blocking her view, until the other girl chuckled. "Seriously. No one will say anything about the fact you're doing the tango with the pride's beta. If we weren't related, I'd probably make a play myself."

"We are not involved." Only because they'd gotten interrupted.

"You mean you're not knocking boots?"

Arabella shook her head.

"Why not?"

"Because I'm not ready."

"Oh. I get it. He's one of those selfish types. I've dated a few. It's all about *them*. Their idea of foreplay is sticking it in you in the alley without a few licks first. Don't they realize a girl needs a little tongue action?"

"Um, I wasn't talking about foreplay." Just saying the word had her blushing. "I meant I wasn't ready emotionally."

Luna seemed so disappointed.

Jeoff, on the other hand, was ecstatic. He paused in his slamming of Hayder's head to say, "You mean this cat hasn't debauched you?"

Arabella shook her head again.

And things might have been okay if Hayder just didn't have to add, "Yet."

The renewed fight might have gone on for another while if a giant of a man, without knocking, hadn't strode in, taken one look at the situation, and stopped it.

The slamming of Jeoff and Hayder's heads together might not have been the nicest way to halt the fight, but it sure proved effective.

"Enough," the big man rumbled.

Both rubbing sore noggins, Hayder and her brother seemed agreed.

The giant tossed a bundle at Hayder, who caught it one-handed.

"You. Get some clothes on before antagonizing Jeoff again."

"And then get out," Jeoff added. "I don't want you near my sister."

"You can't make me stay away," taunted Hayder.

"But I can make it so you both can't talk," the big fellow threatened.

"Spoilsport." Hayder muttered the word under his breath as he took his clothing and left.

Luna left, too, with a cheery, "Thanks for the morning entertainment. That provided a better jolt than a cup of espresso."

Then it was just Arabella, her brother, and the really, really big man, who had just turned his gaze on her.

Given his threats and violent solution, Arabella should have been quaking. At the very least staring at her toes lest she incur his wrath. But the gentlest blue eyes caught hers, and his tone was soft and soothing when he addressed her.

"You must be Arabella. I'm Leo, the pride's

omega."

"More like enforcer," Jeoff muttered, still rubbing his head.

"If you behave, then I don't have to resort to my methods."

"He started it," Jeoff accused, pointing at finger at Hayder, who emerged from the bedroom clad in low-hipped jeans that hugged his corded thighs and a soft T-shirt that clung to his chest.

"Hey, it's not my fault you jumped to the wrong conclusion when I answered the door."

"What else was I to think? You're in my sister's condo wearing only a rag."

"Protecting her."

"The same way you protected her last night when you took her out and flaunted her?"

"I took her to dinner."

"What the hell do you mean you took her out to dinner? You put my baby sister in danger."

"She wasn't in danger."

"They snatched her off the street!"

"And I got her back."

The men glared at each, toe-to-toe, bodies bristling.

Leo, who'd seated himself on a stool by the kitchen island, cleared his throat. "Don't make me get off this stool." The tension remained, but the impending violence moved down a few notches. Seeming satisfied, Leo turned to her. "Coffee?" He addressed that to Arabella, holding out a cup he'd brewed from the machine on the counter.

With a wary look at both Hayder and her brother, she went toward him but then almost scalded herself when Hayder barked, "Baby, where are your pants?"

Oh yeah. She peeked down at her bare legs. To his credit, Leo didn't, but he did smile. "How about I add some sugar and milk to this while you find some pants? You look like you need something sweet."

She couldn't help but return his smile. "Yes, please."

Still ignoring the other two men, she stepped past them to the bedroom, where she scrounged in a drawer for pants. As she dressed, she listened to the arguing.

"She's leaving with me." Her brother hadn't relented.

Neither did Hayder. "Wrong. Arabella isn't going anywhere."

Ouch. She knew her brother wouldn't like that. She was right.

"Excuse me? You don't get a say. She's my sister, my responsibility. I'm taking her."

Arabella stepped back into the living room. "What of the danger though, Jeoff? The pack is in town, and they're looking for me."

"We'll figure something out."

"We already have. She'll stay here with me where she's safe." Hayder crossed his arms over his impressive chest, looking much too determined—and sexy.

A certain brother wasn't impressed. "As safe as she was last night?"

Hayder rolled his eyes. "Oh please. What part of 'we had the situation under control' can you not grasp? Leo, tell the wolf that Arabella was never in any danger."

"I don't lie to my friends," Leo said as he re-handed Arabella her coffee. She took a sip of the hot brew and sighed as she listened to the arguing. When Leo patted the stool beside him, she hopped on.

For such a big man, he offered a strangely calming effect. On her at least. Hayder and Jeoff, on the other hand, just couldn't stem their tirade.

"I was wrong to stick her here. So you can forget I asked."

"Too late. She's part of the pride now."

"She's a wolf, or have you forgotten? She belongs with her own kind." Jeoff crooked his finger at her and inclined his head to the door. Arabella didn't move, more because Hayder's next words froze her.

"She belongs with me. Arabella is my mate."

Chapter Eleven

As conversation stoppers went, it was a good one. The words, 'my mate', hung in the air, and it took a moment for Jeoff and Arabella to explode.

"Hell no!" the wolf yelled.

"No I'm not," Arabella added.

"I think I arrived just in time," Leo announced a second before he grabbed a swinging Jeoff. Leo plopped Arabella's brother onto the couch. "Stay or I'll sit on you."

A wise man—some of the time—Jeoff didn't budge.

"You were told," Hayder taunted.

"Don't make me duct tape your mouth again." Count on Leo to take the wind out of Hayder's sail.

Few people argued with the massive man. Nor did anyone ever tell him to leave, even if Hayder really wished both Leo and Jeoff would go so he could resume the interesting moment he'd shared with Arabella just before all hell broke loose.

Alas, judging by Arabella's guarded expression, that sensual moment was gone. He'd have to find another way to recapture it.

But first he needed to convince Jeoff to let her stay, as well as get Leo to depart—without enforcing an omega-calming moment—and have Arabella lose the rounded shoulders as they fought over her.

Poor baby. How overwhelming this must be for her. How upsetting. And partially his fault.

Shit.

Ignoring the others, Hayder dropped to his knees in front of her. "I'm sorry, baby. Don't get upset. I promise to behave. After all, it's normal your brother would want to protect you, and I shouldn't have beaten the hell out of him for it."

"I think it was the other way around, cat," Jeoff muttered.

"Shhh!" Leo said in a loud whisper. "He's apologizing. Don't ruin it."

Arabella's gaze briefly met Hayder's. "It's okay."

"No, it's obviously not. I can see you're disturbed. You know I didn't mean for that to happen. I never meant to upset you."

"I'm not upset about the fight." Her lips twitched into a small smile. "Boys will be boys, my mom used to say. I'm just sorry to cause all this trouble. Jeoff's right. I shouldn't be here."

"Ha. Told you so." Jeoff crowed in triumph.

"And I shouldn't be with his pack either. With this danger hanging over me, I should flee the country and keep my problems away from all of you."

Leave? He meant to say no, but his lion spoke first. More like rawr-ed.

And in reply? She sneezed. A few times as a matter of fact.

"What's wrong with you?" Jeoff asked his sister.

"Stupid allergies," she grumbled.

Jeoff snickered. "You still suffering from those? That's hilarious. And yet the cat thinks you're true mates?"

"She's mine, and a little sneeze and spit won't change that."

"Is he completely insane?" Jeoff muttered.

"Utterly, but the doctors say he's not a danger to himself or the pride. But I wouldn't push him. And given these two are talking about the future, a future that isn't ours to decide, we should leave them to work things out," Leo politely suggested.

"But—"

Jeoff never got a chance to finish that thought because Leo had spoken. And when Leo spoke, he acted.

"No buts. You. Come." Leo grabbed a hold of Arabella's brother, tossed him over a shoulder, and marched him out with a tossed, "Don't you screw anything up with the girl. I'd hate to have to come back and teach you a lesson."

Had to love Leo—and fear him when he decided to meddle or invite himself places. Although, if a person knew ahead of time he was coming, they doubled their grocery order.

No one wanted to see what would happen if the massive liger—a rare lion/tiger hybrid— ever got hungry. There were rumors about him from his time spent in the army. Rumors that Leo would neither deny nor confirm.

Bastard had the coolest, most mysterious reputation. And yeah, Hayder was totally jealous.

With privacy restored, Hayder turned back to Arabella to see her staring at her toes again.

It irritated him. "Stop it."

"Stop what."

"Stop with the beaten puppy look. You are strong. Hold your head up and show it."

She held her head up all right and shot him a glare. "Would you stop telling me what to do and think?"

"No. Not until you tell me to shove it."

"Shove it."

"Louder."

"Arrrrghhh!" She yelled as she dove on him and tumbled them both to the floor. It resulted in him flat on his back and her straddling him. Awesome.

"That's more like it."

She slapped his chest, not hard enough to hurt him, but enough to show her agitation. Better than her cowed expression. "You are utterly impossible to reason with."

"Never feel like you have to placate me. Speak your mind. We might not always agree, but you should always state your opinion."

"My opinion is you are too full of yourself."

"I am, but if you'll let me, I could make you full of myself."

The innuendo struck gold or, in this case, red, as her cheeks changed color. Her scent changed as well, the musk of her arousal impossible to ignore.

Instead of giving in to her lust—sad meow—she clambered off him.

She then kept her distance from him as best she could as she made herself some breakfast—which he tried to steal from only once. She almost managed to stab him with her fork. After that he wisely left her bacon alone.

Just like he left her alone when she went for a shower.

Even bigger sad meow.

It was pure torture sitting in the living room,

hearing the water running, knowing she stood under its slippery wetness, naked.

She's naked. Without me.

It was enough to drive a lion rabid.

It also made a certain predator antsy. Filled with restless energy—and sexually frustrated—Hayder decided there was only one thing to do. Once she exited the bedroom, squeaky clean—*wanna dirty her*—dressed—*wanna strip her*—and ignoring him—*not for long*—he cornered her in the kitchen.

"Get ready."

Bent over to put some plates in the dishwasher, doing it on purpose he was sure to torture him, she tossed him a look over her shoulder as she asked, "Get ready for what?"

Questioning was good. Not staring at her toes even better. "Does it matter?"

The newer, bolder Arabella narrowed her eyes with suspicion. "Of course it matters."

"Too bad. It's a surprise. You'll have to trust me. Now get some shoes on and grab a jacket just in case. We're going out for a while."

Hair flew in silken strands as she shook her head. "Oh no we aren't. Look what happened yesterday."

"You had fun."

The simple reply stumped her, but not for long. "Fun isn't worth the possibility of yo—um, people getting hurt."

She might have caught herself, but he could guess what she'd almost said. She worried about him. So cute. It made him want to—

Screw want. He acted.

He grabbed Arabella in a big hug, lifted her off

her feet, and planted a big, noisy smooch on her lips.

She squeaked, much like a toy he'd owned as a child, but in her case, he didn't tear her apart to find out where the sound came from. He gently set her back on her feet, even if his true impulse was to drag her into the bedroom and see how many different pitches of squeak he could get her to emit when he explored her body.

She opened her mouth, but he forestalled her with a quickly threatened, "Speak again and I'll kiss you."

"If you're kissing me, then we're not going out. So I guess I win." She flung her taunt at him and crossed her arms, daring him to kiss her, tempting him to kiss, trying to get her way.

Utterly adorable.

But dangerous. If he stayed, he would seduce her, and he knew, while she acted brave now, it wasn't what she wanted. She wanted time, and by the tuft on his tail, she'd get it, even if it almost killed him in the process.

"Baby, you have a wicked side. I like it." He also liked the fact she couldn't protest when he kissed her again as he toted her from the condo to the elevator. He liked that she wound her arms around his neck and growled menacingly enough that, when someone tried to board with them, they changed their mind, leaving them alone.

He kept kissing her, even as he stalked through the lobby, a victim of catcalls, and cat whistles.

Alas, the kissing had to stop once he plopped her into the passenger seat of his car. Driving was best accomplished with his eyes on the road and at least one hand on the wheel.

The other, though, laid claim to her thigh. To

his pleasure, she didn't remove it.

She did, however, start to talk again. "Where are we going?"

"You'll soon see."

"Jeoff won't be happy you're taking me out again."

Like he cared what Jeoff thought. "Hiding you won't make the problem go away. Best we draw your pursuers out in the open and take care of them before we let down our guard."

"You mean you know they might try to follow us?"

He shrugged. "I would assume so. I'm sure they've got people watching the building now that they know where you are. While I don't see anyone tailing us, that doesn't mean they're not there somewhere. But don't worry. Any followers probably have a tail of their own. The pride is on the prowl."

"Aren't you worried someone might get hurt?"

"Don't you dare imply the lionesses can't take care of themselves. They're liable to skin you alive. Literally. They're partial to the furs of their enemies and, given their scarcity in recent decades, eager for any chance to get their hands on some."

"You talk as if the women are equal and as strong as men."

"They are. Sex doesn't determine your ability to defend yourself."

"It can make a difference, especially when it comes to size and strength."

"Physically, yes. And if you are up against someone with no honor, you might be at a disadvantage. But in most cases, simply having the courage to assert your rights is enough to get the respect you deserve. Act like a doormat, and people will step on you. Act as if you have a right to strut, and people will get out of your way."

"Easier said than done."

"No one said it would be easy, but with practice, you'll see it comes naturally. But enough deep discussion. It's time for a little fun. We're here." Turning onto a narrowly paved driveway, lined with conifers that towered at least fifty feet or more, he brought them to a stop in front of a farmhouse, a mansion-sized one, but still a farmhouse.

The structure boasted numerous additions, giving it a unique appearance that had nothing to do with its sparkling white clapboard. The house with its red shutters and front door had belonged to the lions for generations. At one time, they'd lived in it, adding to it as the pride expanded.

Eventually, most of the gang moved to the city, jobs and amenities calling them to a different life, leaving behind only a few permanent keepers. The farm also provided refuge to visitors who enjoyed coming out to the country for a spot of fresh air, a chance to stretch their legs, and a safe spot to unleash their animal side, something they couldn't do in the city.

"What is this place?" she asked as she exited his car and glanced around.

"A place where we can run wild without fear of prying eyes."

"You mean shift." For some reason the saddest expression darkened her features.

He didn't understand. Most shifters were elated at the chance to have a place they could safely run without fear of discovery or hunters. "Yes, shift. We all know how our animal sides love a four-legged run, so

Arik's ancestors created this space for us. It's the Lion's Pride Ranch. Hundreds of acres of woods, fields, and even hills with a river running through it all. To the public eye, it's the place we raise our beef for the restaurants. But in truth, it's a safe zone for our kind."

"Safe how? What makes it different from the national parks?"

"A couple of things. It's enclosed by a fence, ten feet high, electrified and with barbed wire along the top to keep away outsiders. There are cameras monitoring the perimeter along with some pride members, who, I warn you, will take you down if you call them park rangers." Especially if offered a picnic basket. Once again, Hayder spoke from experience.

"Why bring me here though? Even with all those security measures, surely we're safer at the condo?"

"You're with me, which makes you safe. But safety isn't worth squat if you're losing your mind. I thought, with all the stress you've been under, you could use an escape. A chance to run wild and free."

Except the more he talked, the more she withdrew, the more she hunched in on herself. He reached out a hand, but she shied away.

"What is it, baby? What's wrong?"

"We have to leave. Now."

"Are you worried about your old pack attacking?"

"No. Please. We just need to go."

"We're not budging until you tell me why."

The admission, when it came, stunned him. "I can't shift. Not anymore. My wolf is gone."

Chapter Twelve

Admitting her shameful secret aloud hurt, but not as much as the memory of why her wolf no longer came out to play.

She should have known Hayder wouldn't just take her word for it. "What do you mean, you can't shift? You're a wolf. I can smell it."

"I used to be a wolf you mean. Not anymore. I haven't been able to coax my other side out in years. Not even on the full moon." When the urge to shift was strongest.

"Why?"

It occurred to her to tell him to mind his business. She didn't want to admit her shame aloud, but knowing Hayder, and despite their short acquaintance, she knew him well enough to know he wouldn't let it go. Might as well tell him the truth and get it over with. "I tried to escape a while ago. Or, that is, my wolf did. She, that is, we failed. When Harry found me, he and his cronies beat me. Bad. So bad my wolf retreated and hasn't come out since."

For a moment he didn't say anything, and she feared looking at him. Would he finally show disgust at her weakness? Would he finally realize he was mistaken in his belief they belonged together? A man like him deserved someone strong. Someone—

"Would you stop that!" he yelled.

Startled, she raised her head. "I'm sorry."

"Sorry for what? You have nothing to be sorry for."

"But I made you angry."

"Fucking right, I'm angry, baby, but not at you, although I am pissed that you keep looking like I'm going to hurt you every time you talk. The only person I want to hurt is that asshole who did this to you. He's the one I'm angry with. Him and that entire pack of cowards who thought it was okay to let a guy beat on a woman."

His vehemence, far from scaring her, brought a tremulous smile to her lips. "I know you won't hurt me."

"About time you admit it. I am awesome."

Her nose wrinkled. "Is arrogance a lion trait?"

"Nope. That's all me, baby. Now enough about how great I am. Let's get the focus back on you. You're a shifter. No matter what happened to you, that hasn't changed. I'll bet your wolf is just scared to come out. But she doesn't need to be scared anymore. Tell her it's safe to come out."

Her lips drooped. "I've tried communicating with my other half. She doesn't reply. I can't even feel her anymore. It's like she's gone." She didn't mention the fact that she thought she'd heard her whisper a few times since they'd met. She still was trying to convince herself she hadn't imagined it.

"She can't be gone. Let me try. Hey, you, the wolf inside my baby, mind popping out for a bit? Arabella here really misses you."

Nothing.

She shook her head. "I appreciate what you

want to do, but it won't work." How she'd tried and tried to get her furry side to react, respond, anything.

"Maybe she just needs to be reminded of what it's like to run free."

Incomprehension meant she watched as his hands went to the hem of his shirt. He managed to pull it off halfway before she asked, "What are you doing?"

"Getting naked. I hate shifting fully clothed. Shopping for new duds sucks."

"Why are you shifting?"

"To help you, of course."

"What makes you think shifting will help?"

"Your wolf is scared to come out. So my reasoning is it can't hurt to let her see she's in a safe place where she can be herself. And if that doesn't work, then maybe a forest jaunt will."

"You're going for a run?"

"Yup. And you're coming with me."

"I can't come with you. I'll never be able to keep up." Nor did she want the reminder of what she could no longer enjoy.

He didn't pay any mind to her protests. Apparently his lion was bursting to get out. Clothes hit the ground. Naked skin bathed in warm sunlight—and was the object of a much-too-interested gaze. A gaze that did not go unnoticed she realized as her perusal went from his face and dropped lower.

Oh my.

She turned her head and thus missed his transformation. With a rawr that vibrated her bones, Hayder traded shapes, human for fur. He chuffed, an animal sound.

With the temptation of his flesh gone, she dared to look again and then stared. She couldn't help an uttered, "Your lion is beautiful."

And it was. As Hayder stood on four paws, chest proud, head held high, his tail snapped and he shook his head, the feathery fur of his mane ruffling.

Such a majestic beast. Such a conceited one. She caught the wink he tossed her as she stood admiring him.

Needing distraction, she peered around, yet nothing truly grabbed her attention.

Don't stare. He's already got a big enough head. Two of them as a matter of fact.

How was it when she thought of him her thoughts indubitably ended in the dirty gutter running through her mind? She needed something to do with her hands, something other than wanting to stroke his tawny fur and see if it was true that lions didn't purr.

I'd like to stroke him and see for myself.

But she wouldn't.

Stooping to grab his clothes from the ground, Arabella caught the musky scent of his cologne clinging to his shirt, and the sharper scent of his predator.

She sneezed. A few times.

Sigh.

They'd really have to do something about that. Maybe she should look into that shot the doctor suggested years ago.

Look at me, thinking of a future that involves cats. One cat.

One impossibility.

She deposited his clothes in the car, folding them in a neat pile, years of habit where cleaning meant avoiding yet more haranguing. As she shut the vehicle door, Hayder butted his head against her. Practically knocked her over.

He had a pretty big fluffy head.

"What do you want now?"

He stared at her, his eyes questioning.

"No, despite your shifting, my wolf still isn't talking." Although she could have sworn she sensed a second set of eyes spying. Did her inner self watch?

Are you in there? You can come out. It's safe.

Nothing, but the voyeuristic sensation remained.

It seemed Hayder wasn't content with simple admiration. He nudged her again and then did a lazy glide where he ended up alongside her. His tail twitched, thrashing her like a serpentine whip.

"Stop that."

He twitched again, and this time, the tip of his tail tickled the underside of her chin. She craned away. "I mean it. Stop it. I don't know what you want from me. She's not coming out."

Amber eyes, set amidst a shaggy mien, perused her. They seemed to ask something.

She frowned. "I don't understand."

He tossed his head and emitted a soft growl. He wanted something.

"What? What do you want? I'm not shifting. So if you're waiting for me, you'll be waiting a long while. You might as well go for your run. I'll wait for you here." And hope she didn't have to deal with any of her old pack. Hayder seemed convinced this place was secure, but Arabella couldn't halt her doubts.

The buzz of a lone bee kept the silence from being complete. She pretended interest in the mish-mash of additions to the farmhouse. She waited. He waited.

"Daylight's wasting," she reminded.

He didn't leave. Leaning, he brushed his side

against her legs. He chuffed, a whoosh of air and sound.

Surely he wasn't implying she should… "Are you trying to get me to climb on?"

No way. No lion would ever allow himself to be ridden like a pony.

Again, he nudged her.

Say no. This is insane. Don't do it.

Ignoring her inner voice, she swung a leg over his broad back. She straddled him, impressed by his size. Her feet didn't come close to touching the ground. She wobbled atop him when he took a step. Feeling herself losing her balance, her hands shot out and snagged a hold of the first thing she could find.

His mane.

While she did manage to steady herself, she froze, partially horrified. Everyone knew how sacred the mane was to a lion. She'd heard of pack wars started over an insult to a feline's pride and joy.

Yet here she was, using the mane of the beta for the most powerful pride on this coast as a bridle.

He'd eat her for sure.

She held her breath waiting. She also didn't let go, her muscles locked in place.

He didn't buck her off. He didn't snap his mighty teeth at her. He walked.

With a loose-legged stride, he carried her. *He probably just wants to get me out of the driveway before he loses his furry temper and eats me.* Cleaning blood off asphalt and concrete was never any fun. She should know. Poker night with Harry and his cronies had always ended in violence.

They hit the shadow of the forest, the sunlight filtered by green leaves, and still he didn't react to her clinging to his mane.

Was it possible it didn't bother him? Hadn't she seen plenty of examples that Hayder was different from the men she'd known these past years? Time and time again, he kept proving it.

The longer he didn't snap, the more she relaxed. As the tension eased from her, she began to take in her surroundings, the beautiful and peaceful surroundings. How long since she'd gone into the woods?

Too long. It had been years since her last visit to the mini copse in the park that she was allowed to visit when living with her old pack. The supervised outings after her escape had been just another example of the lack of freedom in her miserable life. But even a leering guard was better than nothing. Except nothing was what she got. Either the mini woods didn't appeal or her wolf was well and truly gone. Once she realized her wolf wouldn't come out anymore, she stopped the park visits. Why torture herself?

But how she'd missed the beauty of nature. The quiet serenity of the wild forest surrounded her, a quiet comprised of natural sound. There was always an abundance of that in the world, from the gentle hum of insects to the gentle sloughing of a breeze through branches. What lacked was the chaos of industry and humans.

The abundance of plant life filled her visual senses as the soothing shades of green and brown, interspersed with the occasional startling splash of color, proved a relief after the garish signage and lights of the city.

Best of all was the smell. Could anything really compare to the crisp scent of foliage, a sharp pure tang that screamed life, the fascinating scents of the creatures who lived amongst the roots and branches and then the richness of the earth, musty and yet wholesome. The occasional flower bud provided a hint of sweetness. Such a symphony of flavors.

She inhaled, drawing deep of the fresh air. How wonderful. How—

Miss it so much.

The sudden observation startled her. She stiffened. *Is that you?*

For a moment, she thought her other side wouldn't reply. *Did I imagine it?*

I am here.

Not so much spoken but thought. A communication based less on words and more on that of a feeling.

I thought you were gone. And she'd mourned the loss keenly.

Hiding. Staying out of the way.

But you don't need to hide. We are free now.

Free and you don't need me.

With that, the watching presence vanished, and Arabella almost wondered if she'd imagined the whole thing. Except...

No. She had spoken to her wolf. She was still in there. Wanting to come out, but afraid.

Perhaps Hayder was right. Maybe her wolf needed to be shown it was safe to emerge, to remember the joyful part of being wolf.

Hoping he'd understand, she leaned forward, practically plastering herself to his back, burrowing her face for a moment in his mane, her legs pressing tight against his sides.

Intuitive to her unspoken request, he bounded forward, and she had to tighten her grip. She held on as Hayder ran through the woods. She clung to the muscled and furry back of the lion. She noted the roll of the powerful muscles. Enjoyed the breeze that streamed her hair and that of the lion's mane—which, even though it tickled her face, didn't make her sneeze.

Good thing. One good achoo and she might have flown off his back. Their run took them to the edge of the forest and into a golden field. Swaying stalks extended for acres around.

He dove into them and the whip-like strands tickled at her skin and got caught in her hair. She couldn't help but laugh aloud, all her fear and worries abandoned in that moment as she let a humble wheat field remind her of the simple joys in life.

Remember when we used to play in the fields by our house? I'd hide and Mom would make Jeoff come find me. Her wolf didn't reply, but she could have sworn she listened and remembered the exhilaration of sneaking through the tall strands. Moving carefully so as to minimize noise and movement.

A wolf more stealthy than a fox, or so her brother used to say.

Was she still as tricky as that girl of long ago?

She slid off Hayder's back. He immediately stopped and turned to eye her. A concerned-looking lion was a sight to see. She laughed as she petted him.

"You are such a giant furball. Does anyone else know you're so easy going?"

A lion rolling its eyes; *YouTube* sensation for sure. If only she had a camera.

"I want to play a game." She couldn't believe she said it, but once she did, she didn't regret it. When was the last time she'd let loose and lived a little?

Hayder was right. She'd spent too many years cooped up, a prisoner in her own home, a prisoner of her life and choices. She'd also spent too much time afraid.

Time to live.

"We're going to play wolf hunt. Except, in this case, I guess it's more of a lion hunt, or would that be human hunt?"

He made a noise.

Funny how she could swear she understood him. "Well, I'm human for the moment, so it's apt. Anyhow the name doesn't matter. It's a game I played as a kid with my brother. It was our version of hide and seek. Except we used the wheat and cornfields. And the winner was whoever managed to sneak up on the other and scare the bejesus out of them. Want to play?"

The snort was reply enough.

"When I say go, you close your eyes and count to sixty. Then, come find me."

A laugh fluttered free from Arabella again as he dropped to the ground, ducked his head, and put his paws over it. His tail swished.

Tic. Toc. Damn, she should get moving and not stare at the hypnotic sway of his tuft.

She weaved through the wheat, moving quickly while doing loops and crisscrosses over her path. Anything to muddle her scent trail. She also snagged stray flower weeds on her way. When she had a handful, she rubbed them on herself, her clothes, her skin, masking her scent and matching it to that of the field. Then she circled back, moving toward Hayder's position.

It was a good thing she played close attention because she almost didn't spot him slipping through the waving strands. Only the feathery tips of the wheat and their agitated sway let her know his position, a position she stalked.

And got closer. Closer.

His tail twitched, just in front of her, and the imp in her couldn't resist. She grabbed it and yanked.

Chapter Thirteen

There were a few things that really peeved a lion.

Stealing his sunny nap spot.

Messing up his mane.

Eating the last donut.

Yanking his fucking tail!

Reflex had him spin on the brat who'd sneaked up on him. Well, sneaked up if he ignored the fact he knew she was behind him. Let her think she had him. He was so enchanted by the emergence of a playful side that he didn't want to ruin her fun.

A fun that ended when she yanked his tail.

Rawr!

He spun and shot her a baleful glare.

For a moment she froze. A tremble went through her.

She was scared.

Ah hell. Surely she knew by now he'd never hurt her?

But then again, could he expect years of abuse and habit to disappear after spending just over a day with him? He wondered what she'd do. Would she run or give him the broken puppy eyes?

Why did this have to happen at all? Why did he have to look so fearsome? Was it his fault his lion was so impressive and scary? Was it—

Wait a second, was she laughing?

He eyed her. Yup. She was. Laughing and snorting.

Now he glared for real.

She chortled louder. "Oh. Oh." She gasped. "If only you could see your expression."

He'd show her an expression. He shifted into his human self, but even his impressive nakedness couldn't stem her mirth. He stood and then stalked, each long stride bringing him closer, and her laughter dampening until it stopped altogether. He almost applauded when she peered at him instead of staring at her toes.

"Am I in trouble?"

"Nothing a kiss wouldn't fix." Blackmail? Hell yeah. He'd do anything for a kiss.

"If you want a kiss, you'll have to catch me. Tag, you're it." She shoved him, open-palmed against his chest, before bolting, her lithe body a quick blur that soon disappeared from sight.

Seriously? She was just awesomeness wrapped in a layer of perfection with a dab of naughty he was really loving.

"I'm coming to get you, baby." Off he dashed, a steady lope that would allow her a moment to think she'd escaped. Meanwhile, he'd end up catching her and taking that kiss.

Once he found her. His baby was quick on her feet. Not only that but she didn't move as expected. Her trail moved in a straight beeline, from the field to the edge then the forest.

For a moment, he debated changing shapes again. The fact that she'd left their play area worried him. While he'd told her this area was safe, that didn't mean something couldn't happen.

He needed to find her.

Head angled, he inhaled deeply and caught a whiff of her scent. Faint given her camouflage efforts earlier, but enough for him to follow it to the gurgling stream that ran through this part of the property. He followed her trail, walking the wet, rocky bank, trying to catch a glimpse. He could hear nothing but the rushing fall of water over rocks. He emerged into a vast open area, the roar of water loud now as he stood atop the mini waterfall that fed into an oversized pool.

Still no sign of Arabella. Now he was truly worried. He skipped down the rocks to the edge of the water. Where was she? Had someone taken her right from under his nose? Was she—

Something grabbed his ankles, and he peered down to see a wet Arabella rising from the water, a sea nymph in a bra and panties, grinning in triumph as she yanked his ankles and dragged him in with her.

The cool shock of the water almost had him yelling. He remembered enough to keep his mouth closed until his head broke the surface.

A sleek, wet head popped up alongside him.

"Baby, I am going to make you suffer for that."

"Should I be scared?"

"Very." Because he'd make her suffer the same kind of arousal that plagued him.

Before she could swim away, he snared her and bound her with his long arms. Lucky for him that, while the water proved fairly deep, he could still stand in it and keep most of his upper chest and head above the surface.

Perfect because he had better uses for his energy

than keeping afloat. He'd need it for the kiss he planned on giving her. A long, freaking kiss.

She didn't try to escape his grasp. On the contrary, she wound herself around him, bound him with her legs, tied him with her arms.

Excellent, as it put her in the right spot for him to initiate the embrace. Yeah, baby, claim those lips and devour them.

However, today was a day of surprises. She claimed his mouth first, plastered hers against it, and tugged his bottom lip with her teeth.

From loose to tight, his grip on her changed, his arms binding her to him, especially when the tip of her tongue played with the seam of lips.

While their lips got closely acquainted, their hands didn't remain idle. Hers kneaded the thick muscles that ran across his shoulders. She threaded her fingers through the wet mass of his hair. She ground her sex, clad in wet panties, against his abdomen.

All lovely treats, but he focused more on the exploration of her curves. Once he realized she wasn't going anywhere, he loosened the hug. The water provided a buoyant medium that allowed him to let go so his hands could skim flesh. Down her ribcage his fingers slid to the swell of her buttocks and paused for a squeeze. A perfect handful for gripping. Nice.

He left one hand holding her squeezable ass while the other roamed upward over the swell of her hip and farther up to the lace fabric cupping a perfect peach.

Yes, he would compare her breast to a fruit. Round, firm, with just a little spongy give, succulent to bite into, sweet to the taste, addictive as well.

He couldn't resist.

His hands spanned her waist so he could lift her from the water and position her at just the right height, the right height being where his mouth could tug at the wet fabric until a puckered berry popped out.

It didn't remain exposed for long, not with his mouth immediately covering it.

He groaned. She groaned. They both groaned as he played with the nipple. There were no words exchanged between them, nothing but softs pants and moans of pleasure.

And the splash as something hit the water.

Then another something. The faint echo of a gunshot froze him.

Shit. Someone was fucking shooting at them.

"Take a deep breath," was the only warning he gave before yanking Arabella underwater where they'd prove a more difficult target.

Wide eyes met his under the surface. Kind of hard to explain. Only his great-uncle Clive had ever inherited the famous Johnson gills. Hayder got great hair.

Since he couldn't explain why it appeared he wanted to drown her, he kicked off. With her in tow, he scissor-kicked to the deep end of the pool by the waterfall. Having explored this place many a time when working off some energy, he knew the perfect spot to shelter while he figured out where the shooter was.

And then we'll catch 'em and eat 'em.

It seemed Hayder wasn't the only one peeved at the interruption.

But still…

We don't eat people.

Such a disappointed kitty.

But catch the hunter and we'll order the biggest rare

steak they have in stock.

With the red sauce stuff?

A double order of the red wine reduction, he promised.

Lungs burning, Hayder dragged them to the surface, behind the filtering screen of water cascading from above. The little hidden grotto made a great hiding spot. The shooter would have a hard time targeting them, and the water would also slow the bullet and throw off its aim. He knew they were more or less safe for the moment, but she didn't.

Soaked and scentless didn't mean Hayder couldn't sense the fear coming off Arabella.

She remained tucked close to him, for once not sneezing. Small blessing because one of her ginoromous achoos might have caused quite the amplified echo.

"Was someone shooting at us?" she whispered in his ear. Kind of funny since nothing could be heard above the falling splash of water

"Yes. Someone was trying to get us." Which meant heads would roll with whoever was on duty for security today. Exactly how had someone made it on to pride land with a loaded weapon? What kind of cowards hunted shifters with bullets?

The kind who thought it was okay to beat a woman.

Grrrr.

Man, not lion, made the sound.

It was also the man who made sure to tuck Arabella as deep as he could into the pocket, using himself as a body shield just in case the gunman got a lucky shot.

The crashing of water, not to mention the echoes created by the recess, made it impossible to gauge what happened outside their watery grotto. Did the shooter approach? Did he know where they'd gone? Would he stick around long enough for Hayder to hunt him down and slap him silly?

Only one way to find out.

Submerging himself, he kicked away from the shelter and, with powerful strokes, drew himself to the center of the pool where the water was deep enough for a concealing dive and where'd get the best view of his surroundings.

It also meant, when his head popped from the water, he provided an excellent target.

Rapid splashes showed the bullets hitting the water, one grazing close enough to his ear to flay a strip of skin.

"Shit!" He ducked, but not for long. Shouts erupted, muffled by the water, but still of interest.

Good guys to the rescue or more of the enemy to really fuck with the odds? He let himself float to the surface, allowing only the top of his head and eyes to emerge.

No gunshots, but he did come under a verbal attack.

"I thought cats didn't like water," a voice drawled from the shore.

"I thought you were still in Europe, giving us all a bad name," Hayder replied as he tread water and spun to face the speaker. "What are you doing here?" You being Dean, an old rival. Question was, did Dean work for the good guys or the bad ones?

"Apparently I am rescuing your naked ass from poachers."

"Poachers don't aim at humans."

"Wolves might though."

Wolves? So this was related to Arabella. "You caught the guy shooting at us?"

"Lawrence took care of him while I came to check on you."

"Lawrence is here too?" A buddy of his from back in his college days and then the few years after when he'd taken on a few jobs for the shifter council that led to some interesting missions.

He'd not seen Lawrence in years, which was good, as it meant he got to avoid Dean, the jerk who loved to cockblock so he could steal a chick for himself.

"Forget Lawrence. I'm more interested in this 'we' thing? Who else is out here with you?"

"None of your business."

Wrong thing to say. Dean perked up, and Arabella chose that moment to surface, a sleek water goddess.

A low whistle left Dean. "Well, hello there, sweetheart." Dean showed his stripes—and Hayder didn't mean his tiger ones—with the wide smile he shot Hayder's woman.

"She's taken," he growled in warning.

"No, I'm not," she countered.

Dean's smile widened. "Isn't this interesting."

"The only thing interesting is going to be the sound your face makes when it meets my fist if you don't leave now." Jealousy, Hayder's new best friend. A more level-headed guy might ignore it. Hayder kind of liked it. Rage with a purpose. Awesome.

But Dean ignored Hayder's threat. Instead, he crouched on the rock jutting over the water and beckoned to Arabella. "Come along now, sweetheart. While my buddy Lawrence has taken care of the shooter, with the security system down, who knows how many others might lurk?"

"What do you mean the system is down?" Hayder barked as he outpaced Arabella in the water. This ensured he reached the rock first, and his was the hand she grasped when she arrived a moment later.

He pulled her from the water and wrapped his arms around her shivering frame, less to keep her warm than to ensure Dean didn't get too much of a peek.

While shifters weren't hung up on nudity per se, it didn't mean a lion liked another male ogling his woman.

We could always rip out his eyes.

His lion, ever coming up with awesome solutions.

"You look cold, sweetheart. Here, take this." This was Dean's shirt, which the bastard intentionally stripped to show off his body. Bloody bastard was ripped, of course, and even Hayder had to admit, if he were a girl, he'd probably look. Hell, he was a guy, and he could see how Dean might appeal.

Arabella, though, she didn't ogle the male flesh. Nor did she take the proffered shirt. She shook her head, and even more delightful than her refusal, she ducked closer to him, seeking the haven of his body for protection. A small sign of trust.

He also liked that she wanted nothing of Dean's. However, refusing the shirt meant she was cold and wet. She couldn't hide the shiver that struck her head to toe. That needed fixing. Just not with Dean's scent-marked shirt.

"Where did you put your clothes?"

She pointed a yew yards from them. Hayder stared at Dean, who didn't move.

"Gonna fetch it?" he asked.

Dean arched a brow. "I am not a dog."

"You might not have heard. I'm pride beta."

"My condolences. All that responsibility." Dean shuddered. "I wouldn't want it."

"It's got its perks though, like I get to give people orders."

"Other people maybe. I'm visiting the pride, not part of it. You don't control me. So if you want the clothes, fetch them yourself."

"Don't make me revoke your visitor status."

"Over some broad's jeans and sweatshirt?"

"Men." Arabella sighed before wiggling out of his grasp and stalking to her stashed clothing herself.

A much-too-interested set of green eyes followed her march.

Mine.

Hayder stepped to the left and blocked Dean's line of sight.

A smirk tugged the tiger's lips.

Ignoring it, Hayder focused on more important things such as the news Dean brought. "Tell me more about this security failure." It obviously was linked to the attack on pride land. It was also unheard of. Arik would not be pleased at this grievous breach, and that meant Hayder might get his war after all.

"Before we play one hundred questions, why don't we move to the ATV first? I can tell you the details once we're back at the farm. While I care not a whit for your carcass, it might behoove the woman if we got her somewhere safe just in case there are more gunmen."

The mention of gunmen struck him, and he grasped his idiocy. *Am I trying to get her killed?* Here they both stood, out in the open, perfect targets. *Might as well paint a bull's-eye.* Like a teen with no control, he'd let his irritation and jealousy with Dean cloud his common sense.

Time to get his furry mane back in the game.

Loping toward Arabella, he scanned the area.

"Good god, Hayder. Put some fucking pants on before jogging around balls naked. It's just not right."

Funny how a woman prancing about naked, her luscious tits bouncing was attractive, but a man with his mighty johnson—and yes, the whole johnson nickname started with his line due to impressive girth—had to suffer a lip bitten to prevent mirth.

Before he could slap a hand south to hold it still, she ducked her head. And he'd allowed himself to get distracted again.

Since he saw nothing, he inhaled deeply but didn't sense anything amiss. No unexpected scents. Then again, people with scoped rifles didn't need proximity. The wolves had shown themselves to lack honor when it came to fighting.

As Arabella struggled to pull on jeans over damp skin, he reached her.

"Do you know what's happening?" she asked.

"Not entirely, but enough to know we have to move. There's been a breach on ranch land. The guy shooting at us has been taken care of. However, there could be others. We need to get you to safety." She opened her mouth, but Hayder forestalled her by growling, "Don't you dare say I told you so."

"I would never tell you that."

"But you're sure as hell thinking it." At his words, she couldn't prevent a small smile. "This should have never happened, and when I find out who slacked on the job, my living room will have a new rug."

Clasping her hand once she'd managed to yank on her shirt, he tugged her back toward Dean, who gestured them to where the path through the woods wound. While most of the ranch remained untamed, they still had dedicated trails, perfectly sized for ATVs to get around quickly when out on patrols.

The large machine, red bodied, with big black wheels, a chrome push bar, and mud-spattered side waited, the seat on it perfect for two.

Two people and they were three. Which meant one too many. Ha, and his math teacher said he couldn't mentally solve problems. *See that, Mrs. Klinger. I do not always have to use my fingers.* "There's not enough room on the ATV for all of us."

"Well, isn't that a bit of a pickle. Whatcha going to do? Are you gonna trust me to guard your flank while you drive, or are you going to let your precious lady take a *ride* with me?"

Jealousy screamed at him to take the controls of the vehicle, to have Arabella seated behind him, her arms clamped around his waist. Yet, at the same time, if he shifted to lion form, then he could guard their retreat because, while Dean was good, pride said he was better. And only the best should have the job of keeping his baby safe.

Duty won over jealousy. Barely.

He just gave one low-voiced warning to the wily tiger before shifting. "Try anything and I will kill you." Blunt and lacking elegance but hopefully effective.

As Dean straddled the ATV and gestured for Arabella to clamber on the back, Hayder swapped skin.

Instantly his senses sharpened. Everything became clearer, more defined. His nose twitched as it sorted the myriad scents. His eyes roved constantly, searching for motion. His tail swished, more because he liked the feeling than for any true purpose. The ATV rumbled off, Arabella gingerly perched on the back, hands clasping Dean's shirt, but holding herself away from his body.

It appeased the beast.

Still gonna rub on her. His beast's solution when it came to ensuring she wore the proper scent. But at least rubbing was better than peeing. Yeah, he'd heard the story of Luna's ex and his weak bladder.

Keeping the glimpses of Arabella's shirt within sight, Hayder shadowed their retreat, all senses on high alert. His ears pricked forward, straining for sound. When he encountered shadowy concealed pockets in the forest, he plunged into their hearts, seeking out possible enemies. They proved empty and harmless, although he did scatter bunnies in one instance, big, fat, fluffy ones that tempted his feline side.

Not the time to hunt for dinner. Hunt for intruders.

Ahead he ranged, in search of danger, but other than the peril Dean posed if he laid a hand on Hayder's woman, they made it back to the farm safely.

Such a shame. His poor disappointed lion sulked his way back to his spot inside Hayder. Feline shifters had it so much easier than others, their cat sides fairly mellow creatures who didn't mind quick jaunts out to play followed by long periods of rest—rest atop a soft pillow bathed in sunshine.

A few other all terrain vehicles were parked in front of the farmhouse, and Dean pulled his alongside. Arabella immediately hopped off, and though bodies milled, her gaze sought him out. Was it conceited for him to believe he could see relief loosening the tension in her body once she spotted him?

"Hayder. Dude. You seem to have lost your pants," said one of the guys hanging out. Given the gathering of shifters, this comment didn't draw as much attention as it might elsewhere. He took a moment to scan the crowd. Dean, of course. A few of the ranch caretakers—Polly, Ken, Horace. Then there was Lawrence, still straddling an ATV, sporting a very unconscious wolf slung over the back of the machine.

Given the entertainment he'd provided earlier with his johnson and jumping jacks, Hayder took a moment to grab his clothes and dressed before joining everyone. He sidled up alongside Arabella who stood just outside the group discussing what they'd found— not damn much.

To his irritation, she didn't stand alone. Dean purposely flanked her. Did he hip check a little harder than needed—and used both hands for propulsion—to shove Dean out of the way? Yeah. And it worked.

He took the spot beside Arabella, his manhood appeased.

And then torn to shreds as Arabella erupted into sneezes. Great big, body-shaking ones. She moved away, and they subsided.

Dean dared to laugh. Hayder gave no warning. His fist moved of its own volition and somehow found its way to Dean's face.

Smack.

The uncontrollable spasm barely budged the big tiger, but Dean did rub his jaw and shoot him a baleful glare. "What the hell was that for?"

"Muscle twitch." Hayder shrugged in apology and almost laughed as Dean growled. But the other man knew better than to start shit with the pride's beta, especially in front of witnesses.

"How many teams are still out in the field?" Hayder asked as he counted heads and realized a handful were still missing.

"We've got three more teams out. One was chasing another pair of wolves but ran into problems when Darcy got tranquilized."

"The intruders were shooting darts? Even the one Lawrence captured?"

Still sitting astride his ATV, Lawrence held out a rifle in one hand, a pair of tufted missiles in the other. "This is what I found on the guy I caught. I used it on him, and it knocked his ass out hard, but he's still breathing."

"So they didn't want to kill you."

"Hey, do you think those sorority girls are back in town?"

And before anyone think he changed the subject, it should be noted a few years back that he'd caught the eye of a few tigresses. Aggressive young ladies who had drugged him, and when he awoke, let's just say their idea of pain and torture involved feathers and edible oils.

"Use your head, Joey. Why would those gals send in a wolf to do their job?"

Poor Joey had to ponder that one.

Hayder almost sighed aloud. "The wolves are here because of Arabella. There's some kind of thing going on with her old pack. I'm surprised you hadn't heard."

Dean frowned. "We did but didn't think much of it. What kind of idiots would come after a girl and provoke a war?"

"A pretty fucking brazen bunch of Lycans if you ask me." Lawrence didn't mince words.

"So what does this mean?"

Hayder might have stared at their prisoner when he spoke, but all he saw was his baby, in danger.

Not happening.

"This means it's time we showed them they chose the wrong pride to mess with." The hunt was on. *Rawr.*

Chapter Fourteen

The urge to hide persisted.

Hide. Before you get hurt. Protect yourself.

Instead of bolting off, Arabella hugged herself, but it couldn't stem the trembling inside.

For a moment, with Hayder in the water and field, she'd let her guard down. She'd allowed herself to frolic as if she didn't have a care in the world. She should have known better. Karma didn't use a gentle hand when she slapped her for her temerity. *How could I have forgotten the drama that follows me? The violence.*

A violence that threatened Hayder.

Don't hurt him. Or else…

How aggressive her thinking when it came to his safety, and yet, when hers was threatened, she wanted to run, or hide, anything to avoid the possibility of pain.

She should have been on guard, not frolicking.

But it felt so nice.

It had. So nice to run and play. But nicer still than that was the kiss she'd shared with Hayder. A kiss so scorching, so right, it would have led to them making love, of that she was certain.

She could protest all she wanted that she wasn't ready for any kind of relationship. Yes, it was too soon. And yes, her life was a mess. It didn't matter. When Hayder touched her, all she wanted was more. More of him. His touch. His affection.

I want it all.

The attack put a stop to that foolishness. *No happy ending for me.* The pack showed a determination even she hadn't expected. Their tenacity also appeared to surprise Hayder, who took in the evidence of their planned attack with brows that kept inching upward until they practically disappeared under the hair flopping over his forehead.

"What do you mean they managed to knock out our fucking cameras?"

"They blew the transformer up the road. We lost all power."

"What about the goddamn generator?" Hayder asked.

"It didn't kick in like it was supposed to. We're taking a look at it now to see what's wrong with it."

Hayder scrubbed a hand over his face and made a growl of frustration. "They planned this attack out well. Too well, which makes me wonder if you had no eyes and ears, then how did you know to come to my aid?"

Dean cleared his throat. "We didn't, but I figured something fishy was afoot when both systems went down at once. I volunteered with Lawrence and the others to do a perimeter scout. That's how we found you pinned down by that wolf."

"His name is Sam," Arabella offered.

"You recognize him?"

Uneasy at the focus of so many eyes, Arabella fought an urge to flee. Hands clasped tight and forcing herself to keep her chin up, she nodded. "I don't know him well, but I have seen him before. He's pack beta to the High Hills Pack." What she didn't understand was his motive.

Hayder obviously wondered as well. "What the hell is the beta from the High Hills Pack doing here? He's far from home. And pretty fucking ballsy attacking us on pride land. When he wakes up, Sam's going to have some questions to answer. Any chance he's working with your old pack, baby?"

"Baby." Dean snickered and also danced to the right when Hayder did a side lunge where his arm shot out, fist closed.

He missed and, much like a cat, pretended nonchalance as his extended arm rose and Hayder mimed a stretch.

She fought a smile. "I guess these guys could be working with my old pack. But I don't see how. They've been rivals for years."

"Maybe your pack asked for help?"

"I doubt it. My pack isn't the type to ask anyone for help."

But as it turned out, help wasn't why Sam attacked. While Arabella was tucked in a kitchen being fed and regaled with stories by some of the resident lions, Hayder and some of the other felines were questioning their prisoner. By what means, she didn't ask.

Sympathy was for victims, not strangers who attacked her.

Whatever the answers, Hayder emerged grim faced and his order to, "Get in the car. We're heading back to the city," emerged clipped.

Tires spun gravel when he took the sharp right turn onto the main road back into the city. She kept quiet, hands gripping her seat. Hayder practically vibrated in the grips of emotion. Not just any emotion;

anger.

Not good. Not good. Never good.

She knew what happened when men got angry and needed an outlet.

Hayder growled. "Don't be afraid."

"I'm not," she lied.

"Those guys won't get close to you again. I'm sorry. I fucked up earlier. It won't happen again."

"You're apologizing?" Her mouth rounded into an O, and that easily, all her fear melted. How could she ever think Hayder would hurt her? He wasn't Harry. He wasn't like the men in her old pack. "You're not the one who has to apologize. I am. For a moment, I forgot what you'd shown me so far and lumped you in with the jerks from my pack."

His lips tightened. "Don't ever compare me to them. I am nothing like those honorless curs."

"I know, which is why I apologized. Next time you look that pissy, I'll tell you to chill."

"Pissy? I was raging. Incensed. Nothing so emasculating as pissy."

"You are a very strange man, Hayder."

"It's called fascinating, baby. Just think of all the cool levels of me you still get to learn about."

"I don't suppose there is a modesty one in there somewhere?" She couldn't help but tease, especially since his answering grin sent such a warm feeling through her.

"Honesty is one of my virtues. No point in hiding the truth. I am awesome."

Again, he made her laugh, but the light mood between them couldn't last, and she was the one to wreck it by asking for more of the truth.

"Why were you so angry?" she ventured.

His expression was hard to read, and not just because the shadows in the car draped him, with only the occasional other cars on the ride illuminating him for an instant. He drove one-handed, his left hand casually gripping the steering wheel. His right arm shifted from the armrest, and his hand landed firmly on her thigh. He squeezed the leg, nothing sexual, but more of comfort. A, 'Hey, I'm here, so don't freak out'.

"I need you to not get scared if I tell you."

"That bad?" She waited for a tremor, but with Hayder's warm hand on her, she remained relaxed.

"Depends on what you think is bad. Seems that Sam fellow attacked us by order of his alpha."

"Are they insane?" The exclamation burst from her, but she didn't worry that he would punish her. She was beginning to understand Hayder wasn't just a different breed of shifter, but of man too. One who welcomed dialogue and opinions, even from a woman.

"Obviously they're a few screws loose, but it seems their bigger motivation is greed. Or more accurately, a hunger for money and power." He turned his glance from the road to fix her with a golden stare. "Just how much are you worth, Arabella?"

Shifting in her seat, she couldn't hold his gaze and, instead, stared at the twisting fingers in her lap. "Let's just say that the lawyer said I'd never have to work and I could live as lavishly as I wanted and probably not make much of a dent."

A low whistle came from him. "Add to your wealth the role of alpha for your old pack and you've become not just a prize for the males in the Northern Lakes but just about every pack for several states around. The Lycan Council"—a separate group from the High Council that ruled all the shifter groups—"has declared the Pack Challenge open to all contenders."

"Why would they do that?"

"They cited a need for a different direction in leadership. Apparently they don't think the pack had anyone suitable for the position. By making it open to all, they're hoping to bring in new blood and perpetrate a shakeup."

"That's all good and well, but what does this have to do with me?"

"The Lycan Council wanted to sweeten the pot, so they tossed out the fact you were an heiress."

"They made me a freaking prize?" She'd gotten used to being treated as a possession by Harry, but to actually have a band of people condemn her like that, as if she were no more than an object for bartering? It hit her hard. *I mustn't let them hurt me.* She must have uttered the words aloud because he answered her.

"Don't take it as an insult, baby. Yes, you are a prize, a priceless, precious one. I'd do all manner of things to keep you safe. And I wouldn't do it because of your wealth or the alpha position. You are the most valuable thing."

Was it hot in the car because she was suddenly melting. Never had someone said something so utterly beautiful to her.

"You say all the right things."

"I don't just say, baby. I act. You'll see over time."

"If I have time."

"You'll get that time. Don't you worry." The tight squeeze of her thigh provided some reassurance, but it was his vehement words that warmed her most of all. "I won't let them take you, baby. I'll tear them apart, barehanded, if I have to."

"For how long, though?" How long would she have to live with this threat hanging over her? Would the Lycan packs stop once a new leader was chosen on the full moon, or would they keep coming after her, determined to get their grubby paws on her wealth? "I don't want to spend my life hiding or flinching at shadows."

"We could end it all right now." His words, spoken as he rounded the curve of the road bordering a cliff, didn't prove reassuring.

Arabella's hands clutched at her seat as she stared at the dizzying height. *Surely he's not implying…* "I don't think I'm ready to die."

Laughter filled the car, low and husky, and she wanted to hope not the evil kind of cackle before he jerked the wheel and sent them soaring off the cliff. "Oh, baby, not that kind of end. I meant we could end wolf business by making you unavailable. If you're already claimed, then they'll have to ditch their efforts."

"Claimed? By who?"

He snorted. "You really have to ask? I told you this morning, and I'm telling you again. You're my mate."

How right it sounded when he said it, but wasn't she the naïve girl who'd once believed another smooth-talking man? "How can you be sure? We're not even the same species."

"And?"

"I'm allergic to you."

"But already getting better. Look at us, together in a car and you've yet to sneeze once."

How quickly he'd forgotten her fit earlier when he hugged her before going off to question Sam. She noted he no longer wore the same shirt—a result of too many sneezes or blood from the interrogation?

"Mixed matings have problems with infertility." Children, something she'd worked hard to not have with Harry. Unbeknownst to her dead mate, she had an IUD inserted. While she had resigned herself to her fate, she refused to subject an innocent to it.

"So we'll adopt. Or live vicariously through other people's kids. The pride has an abundance of ankle biters for us to spoil and borrow. I know Aunt Hilda would love to dump a few of her progeny for a while so she could get a break."

He made it so simple. Tempting. "You have an answer for everything."

"Except for the one thing I've asked. Will you be my mate?"

A firm nip of her tongue allayed the Yes! She shouldn't jump into this. She needed time to think. "What if I say no?" Would he force her?

"Then I shall yowl outside your door and haunt you with big kitty eyes until you break down and scream yes. Which, by the way, you'll also scream when we finally get alone and I finish what we started today."

Way to remind her about the kiss. That decadent, scorching kiss. Oh my.

"I—I—" The proper answer to his question of 'Will you be my mate?' was no. She could enumerate so many valid arguments about why she should refuse. And yet…she wanted to say yes.

He's ours. We should claim him.

As if she'd listen to the half of herself that chose to hide from the world.

I must hide. Better that way. Everything is my fault.

Arabella might have questioned further, but they slowed to a stop in front of the condo, and a valet in uniform held open her door.

Then she was surrounded by cats. Excited cats who pounced on her with questions.

"Is it true someone attacked you at the ranch?"

"Has anyone laid dibs on the wolf they caught?"

"Does this nail color make my fingers look fat?" That question wasn't thrown at her specifically but in general. But it was the only one Arabella had an answer to.

"I think it's pretty."

"Ladies. If you don't mind, Arabella needs to rest after her harrowing escape. But be on your guard. Patrol vigilantly. The wolves have declared war, and we need to show them why that was a stupid fucking idea."

Cheers met his announcement.

Hayder wrapped an arm around her waist and steered her through the curious crowd. The noise, friendly as it was, reminded Arabella how different the pride was from the pack.

"Are the women always like this?"

"Like what? Loud? Meddling? Violent? Yes to all three." How proud he sounded.

"It doesn't bother you?"

He frowned. "Why would it bother me? They're just being themselves. It might drive me nuts at times, and privacy is something they don't respect, but that's what makes them so precious to me. To each other. We respect our different personalities. We encourage strength, especially when it comes to family. We aren't only a lion's pride. We have pride. Rawr."

His mock roar made her smile. "You make it sound so simple."

"It is. We are. Which is why you belong with us. Or more specifically with me."

Unrelenting was another trait the lions had in abundance. Hayder seemed bound and determined to have her agree to become his mate.

The question was, did she dare?

A long time ago, she'd thought she understood the choice. She'd messed up.

But admit it, you saw the signs. You just chose to ignore them.

Just like, for the moment, she had to ignore him in order to think.

As she closed the bedroom door, leaving Hayder—and the temptation he proved—behind, she leaned against the portal and couldn't help flashing back.

Yes, she'd seen signs Harry had a darker side. His quick temper when things didn't go his way. The rude and sexist remarks that she chose to ignore.

However, his true vicious streak didn't emerge until he'd conned her into marrying him and then taken her back to the bosom of his pack.

The first slap because his bacon was overcooked proved a shocker. The first beating because she dared tell him she didn't like his treatment even more so.

Please don't hurt me.

A plea that shamed her and accomplished nothing.

But it was a reminder that she couldn't trust her judgment. She shouldn't rush.

And it was with those thoughts circling in her head that she fell asleep—and dropped into her nightmare.

Chapter Fifteen

Hayder paced Arabella's living room. It killed him to know she was alone with her thoughts. He could see the turmoil in her, a turmoil he'd hoped to remove by asking her to be his mate.

Except she didn't reply. She left him in limbo, wondering what she thought and felt.

Does she care for me?

He could swear she did. The recollection of how she'd melted in his arms by the waterfall quickly aroused him. For just a moment, he'd gotten a glimpse of the Arabella hidden within, the free spirit with a passion for life.

A passion for him.

She desired him. No doubt about it, but she was so damned scared he'd turn into a dick that she held back.

Give her time. She was right when she said she barely knew him. Only days since they'd met. Enough time for him to jump into this mating with two damned feet and a hell yeah. She on the other hand, dragged her feet.

But she was coming around. Already the timid, trembling creature he'd first met showed signs of snapping out of her shell. He just needed to give her time.

Time alone, which meant him on the damned couch again—sad meow—with a freaking erection that wouldn't go away.

Maybe he should try a cold shower? Or, even better, the cold reality of a ringing phone, which, when answered, released a barked, "Where the fuck are you?"

"On the couch. Where are you?"

"In my condo waiting for you to report."

"Please, like you don't know every single detail already. Besides, I needed to make sure Arabella was okay."

"Is she?"

"Yeah." Physically maybe, but emotionally, they still had a ways to go.

"She'll be fine here. Sic Luna on her while you pop up for a bit."

"No. I'm going to take your advice and, instead of running to you all the time, start using the phone. Like right now. Hey, boss, this is your beta reporting in." He resisted the urge to make a staticky sound and add, 'Big Kitty out'. His code name when he used to work in the field before getting called to the pride to take over the duty of beta.

"Hayder, you are really tempting me to march down there and kick your ass."

"But that would mean leaving Kira all alone, and so late at night. I know she goes to bed early. Do you really want to waste that much time when we could just hash it out on the phone?"

A sigh. "Fine. Lay it on me. I heard a few stories, but I want it from your perspective."

"We were attacked."

"I still can't believe they dared!" The roared words practically vibrated the phone Hayder held against his ear.

"Yeah, you and me both. But the fact is the Lycan Council decided to paint a pretty big bull's-eye on Arabella's back."

"A barbaric target that I can't believe the Lycan Council even condoned," Arik growled. "I've deposited a complaint with the High Council."

But would that panel of sages reply in time to stop things from escalating further? At this point, it was war.

Lion against wolf. Things would get ugly unless...

"I've got a solution," Hayder ventured.

"Kill them all and show them why you don't mess with a Lion's Pride." The ladies downstairs would have cheered for sure, but Hayder saw the flaw in the plan.

"Good plan, except for all the blood and bodies." In this modern age, making people disappear wasn't as easy, not when government entities like the IRS came looking for them and cops had access to science to solve crimes. "Actually, I was thinking if Arabella wasn't available then they'd have to stop their attacks."

"You want to kill the girl? I thought you liked her."

He snorted and rolled his eyes. "I do like her. And I was not implying I'd kill her. What is it with you and Arabella thinking that's the only viable solution? I'm talking about claiming her."

"You mean you want to marry the girl?" A sigh of relief. "Well, that makes more sense, if a tad drastic. Must you really resort to the ball and chain? Ouch." A hand muffled the receiver, but Hayder still heard. "Calm down, mouse. I only meant it as a joke. I love being mated." Arik laughed as Kira threatened him with wax strips. The hand over the mouthpiece shifted as Arik came back on the line. "Okay, so you marry the girl. Are we sure that will stop them? They could decide to kill you and take her."

"Kill me?" Hayder snorted. "No need to be insulting."

Arik chuckled. "Sorry. Couldn't help myself. But more seriously, just claiming her might not be enough. Look at the depths they've gone to already. This is more than just one or two guys coming after Arabella. This is a group effort, and as such, we need to take more precautions, especially as they've infiltrated our territory."

"Time to flush them out?"

"Yes. We need to make an example of those daring to think they can strike with impunity. We must show no mercy if we're to prove our strength to the other packs and prides watching."

For a few minutes, they discussed strategy. Basically, it boiled down to let the lionesses loose to have them track the wolves that didn't belong to Jeoff. Then, so long as they didn't get caught or leave any evidence behind, free rein to do as they pleased.

That was as far at they got. The finer details would have to wait. A whimper came from the bedroom.

This time Hayder was ready for it. "Gotta go."

He hung up on Arik and tossed his phone on the couch before making a beeline for the bedroom. The door had been repaired while they were out, but it took only a firm kick to splinter the jamb and give him entry.

He didn't waste time stripping, although he did shed his shoes before climbing into bed with Arabella. She thrashed under the sheets, her face drawn into a rictus of pain and terror, her breath panting and rife with mewls of panic.

Into his arms he drew her trembling body, holding her tight against him until the tremors in her eased. He brushed his lips across her brow and continued even once her breathing evened out.

He knew the moment she woke because she stiffened in his arms then relaxed.

"Hayder?"

"Expecting someone else?"

"Just making sure since I'm not sneezing."

He couldn't help but laugh at her unexpected teasing words. "I told you the more time we spent together, the more you'd get adjusted."

"Did you break the door again?"

"You shouldn't have locked it."

"I didn't."

"Oh." He'd never thought to check. "Oops?"

He loved her small laugh. "I better not get a bill."

"Don't worry. We have a maintenance crew as part of the amenities that come with the building. Some of the pride can get a little rambunctious, so repairs are pretty much a daily thing around here."

She didn't reply and several minutes passed. She remained in his arms, her warm body clad, once again, in only a thin T-shirt and panties. So little to separate. His own layer of clothes added a barrier. However, that didn't stop the heat building between them.

How he needed her.

Time to work his wiles. "We should talk about

the mating thing again. Essentially the pros." Pro number one, she got him. Funny how he'd wager that same pro headed the top of the list for cons.

She sighed. "Can't we just stay like this for a while?"

"You can have this forever if you just say the word." Tenacious, that was him.

"How's the word maybe?"

He blinked. His lion blinked. He mulled her reply and finally blurted out, "Maybe? That's all I get?" A tad insulted? Try a truckload.

"I like you. A lot. But I'm scared. Scared of making the wrong choice again. Everything is moving so fast. I feel like I barely know you. And yet, at the same time, I feel like I've known you forever. A part of me wants to say yes. But..." She trailed off.

His turn to sigh. "But you need time."

"I do, but I don't know if I'll get it. Not with the way the packs are after me."

"They won't get you. If you need time, then I'll get you some damned time. I don't want you to say yes because you feel like you have to. I want you to say yes because you want me."

"I want you." The admission made him utter a silent mental roar. "I just don't know if I can handle forever yet."

"Then let me give you a for-now."

"What's a for-now?"

He showed her, dipping his head until he could brush his lips across hers. Her breath caught. He kissed her again, this time keeping contact with her the entire embrace. With a soft sigh, her lips parted, and he tasted her, teased her, their tongues twining in a sinuous dance.

Her body arched against him, and he reveled in

it. He slid his hand from where he'd stroked her back in slow circles down to her full bottom. Her breathing hitched as he slid his hand under the fabric and cupped the soft flesh within.

"We should stop now," she murmured between kisses.

"Or you can trust me. Let me please you."

"But—"

His lips traveled from her sweet lips to the shell of her ear where he whispered, "No claiming. Just pleasure. Trust me, baby."

"I want to trust you."

"Then let me show you how it can be." He tugged at her lobe with his teeth.

She gasped when Hayder kneaded the flesh of her ass, the flesh soft and silky. How he wanted to sink his teeth into it and nibble.

Mmm, thinking of nibbling, he couldn't help but recall a perfect set of berries he'd tasted that afternoon.

Wanna taste again.

He rolled her onto her back and let his hands skim her shirt upward until they exposed her luscious breasts. With one hand, he cupped the perfect globe, his thumb brushing over the peak. It puckered in response, a hard nub begging for a suck. He dipped in for a taste.

He took her whole nipple and part of her breast in his mouth, tugging and sucking at it while soft cries panted past her lips.

No need to touch her between the thighs. He knew her cleft moistened. He could smell her musky arousal and feel the tremble of her legs as she reacted to his touch.

He nipped the tip of her nipple, and a shiver went through her. Another gentle nibble and she was clasping his head, moaning.

She wasn't the only one who wanted to moan. His cock throbbed, begging to be let loose. But he'd made a promise. A promise he wasn't sure he could keep if his cock went anywhere near her flesh.

This is about her. This is about showing her she can trust me and my word, no matter how hard it is. And damn was it hard.

He let his hands roam her body as his mouth returned to capture her lips and soft cries. He tickled her delicate skin with the rough texture of his fingers. He rasped his digits along her taut nipples, she inhaled a sharp breath, and he smiled, even as he continued the embrace.

How responsive she was. So perfect.

Across the gentle rounding of her belly he stroked, moving ever downward, noting how her heart raced and the moment she held her breath when his fingers encountered the edge of her panties.

She froze as he dipped under the elastic and touched the curls on her mound.

"Do you want me to stop?" He would if she asked. He might die, though, if she did.

"Yes. No. I—I—"

Confusion reigned as her mind told her one thing while her body screamed another.

"Keep trusting me, baby. This is all about you. And only you."

In reply, she dug her fingers into his shoulders and plastered her mouth against his. She kissed him. She inserted her tongue into his mouth and drew a groan.

For a moment, he let himself get distracted. He rolled his body atop hers, fully clothed. Her thighs spread wide to accommodate him, and he groaned again as he pressed his hidden arousal against her sex. Braced on his forearms, their lips melded, he rubbed against her, teasing strokes that even with them both clothed still titillated.

The friction was delicious. The aroma of her arousal decadent. The moisture that soaked her panties and then seeped through his jeans tempting.

Arabella mewled against his lips, her panting breath hot and erratic. She clung to him, her fingers digging into the muscles of his shoulders as her pleasure mounted.

Hers wasn't the only pleasure cresting. He had to stop now, or he might not be able to keep his promise.

Tearing his mouth from hers, he reared up and spent a moment staring down at her. Lips swollen, cheeks flushed, eyes heavy with passion.

"You are so beautiful, baby," he growled. The most beautiful woman he'd ever seen. *And she's mine.*

His to kiss. Touch. Taste.

Mmm. Taste...

Sliding back on the bed, he positioned himself so he knelt still between her legs but farther down. He felt her watching him as he tugged at her panties, dragging them down until they got caught around her knees, his body in the way. Fuck it.

It took but a simple wrench to rend the fabric and toss the scraps aside.

She gasped, but he was pleased to know it wasn't in fear. Oh no. Anticipation and arousal were what made her chew at her bottom lip and made the flesh between her legs glisten with honey.

Taste her. Lick her.

Basic needs. Primal needs. He ignored them

both. This wasn't about him. He wanted to show her pleasure, the kind that came from a man who wanted to worship.

With that thought in mind, he teased her by rubbing the bristled edge of his jaw along the silky skin of her inner thigh.

She shivered.

He did it again, this time to the other side.

She made a mewling sound.

He poised his mouth before her exposed pink sex, letting his warm breath brush against it. She let out a cry, and her hips jerked.

"Hayder!" She moaned his name, her need so clear he could hold off no longer. His lips latched onto her sex with a suddenness that made her exclaim, and her whole body arched.

But he followed her bucking hips and kept lapping at her core, spreading her pink lips to delve within. He stabbed her with his tongue and held her hips tight as he foraged. She trembled in his grasp. Her body. Her sex. Even her breathing wavered.

When he let his lips move to her pleasure nub, she let out a small scream. She was close, so close. He flicked her clit with his tongue and, at the same time, inserted a finger into her.

How tight she felt. How hot. He inserted a second one, even as he continued to tease her swollen button.

She thrashed on the bed, her upper body at least. He held her hips pinned to the bed as he pleasured her. In and out, he thrust his fingers, feeling her tightening around him, the walls of her sex pulsing with heat and tension.

Faster he stroked. Faster. Faster...

She came. Her whole body froze in a perfect arch that saw her back rounding away from the bed, her whole body one taut plane. Her sex shuddered as waves of bliss shook her. Her scream was strident. Loud. Unabashed.

And did he say loud?

He had only a moment to spring to his feet and toss a blanket over Arabella before he confronted a snarling lioness, whose roared, "Die, wolf," faded to an, "Oops. My mistake."

A smirk on her lips, Luna waggled her fingers goodbye and then left.

Hayder almost stalked after her but was stopped by…laughter? He spun around to confront the source. Arabella giggled, quite uncontrollably too.

Arms crossed over his chest, he tried to appear stern. "I fail to see the humor."

"That's because you can't see the look on your face."

He'd wear that look every day if it meant hearing her laugh. He could also get used to seeing her like this everyday. Damned she looked good. Despite the sheet drawn to her neck, Arabella still appeared the perfect picture of passionate decadence with her tousled hair, swollen lips and still flushed countenance.

Wanna snuggle.

It wasn't just the lion that wanted to crawl into bed with her and spoon. It occurred to him that the ill-timed interruption had stolen his after-moment. It also brought forth one of the pride's most annoying habits. Meddling, even if well intentioned. "Sorry about the interruption."

Her lips quirked. "Does it happen often?"

To lie or not to lie. "Unfortunately yes."

Privacy wasn't often respected in the pride. They were families. Families butted in. And fights broke out. Reunions and holiday feasts were always an event—requiring a few first aid kits.

Good thing they kept a few were-lions on the police force to smooth over any disturbance complaints.

Locks meant nothing. Neither did knocking. So was he surprised that someone came barging in because he'd made Arabella scream too hard? And, yeah, that tidbit did render him a tad smug.

Truthfully, he should probably thank Luna for her diligence. It meant she'd accepted Arabella as part of the pride, and as such, that meant she'd protect her.

But who would protect his poor abused balls from his baby?

Crooking a finger, she beckoned him. Crawl back in bed and try to keep his mind off sinking his hard cock into her sweetness, or take a really cold fucking shower—while giving himself a hand job to better help him keep his promise to her of not claiming her before she was ready.

He chose pure torture. He crawled back into bed with her.

Was the "Eep," that escaped him as the touch of her burrowing against him very manly? No, and neither was his feline very supportive considering it did a flop and stuck its legs in the air, lolled its tongue, and pretended it was cartoon dead.

Very fucking funny.

But true. It might kill him having her spooned so close, and him promising to not claim her. Yet, how could he refuse her when she said, "Will you sleep with me and keep the nightmares away?"

He uttered a mournful second "Eep" as her

buttocks fitted against his groin, but he used the torture as a strengthening exercise all the while thinking, *my woman, mine*, as he held her in his arms.

Chapter Sixteen

This is nice.

More than nice. Waking up in the arms of a man who made you feel protected, instead of on edge and tense, proved amazing.

Hayder was amazing.

What man would forgo his pleasure even though he surely smelled her erotic interest? Hayder had. While he might have let his evident erection rub against her, he did nothing else.

Nothing.

At all.

He didn't press her, the jerk. However, he did torture with what could happen. Her mind didn't help by rerunning the pleasure he'd given her. A pleasure she wanted more of because one climax at his hands acted like a drug. One hit and she wanted more.

I want him.

He's ours.

The echo in her psyche no longer surprised her as much. It seemed a certain dormant part of her stirred. After so much time, Arabella just needed to have some patience. Give her wolf time to heal and adjust.

The dark room belied the red glare of the numbers on the clock. "How can it be seven thirty a.m. and pitch-black in here? I usually get great morning sunlight."

Lips nuzzled the back of her neck, firing a shiver down her spine. She squirmed in retaliation, rewarded by a groan as a length of molten steel pressed against the seam of her butt. "I had them put in blackout curtains while we were at the farm yesterday."

She froze. For some reason, his assumption that he'd sleep with her stung. Was she such a pushover? Had she learned nothing? Even worse. He'd guessed right.

They had slept together, and while they hadn't had sex, she'd definitely let him take extensive liberties with her body.

Hell, I would have had sex with him if he'd pressed me.

But that wasn't the point. How dare he be so arrogant as to premeditate something that should happen naturally over a course of time as a man and woman got to know each other? "You mean you assumed you'd be sleeping in here?"

"Of course. I'm your mate, even if I haven't claimed you yet. Where else would I be?"

"On the couch."

"But it's short."

"How about in your own apartment?"

Out of bed she rolled, to her feet, ignoring his, "Where you going, baby?"

"For a shower—"

"Awesome."

"Alone."

"There's room for two."

She spun, chin held high, and while her challenging stare was rusty from lack of practice, she threw it on as she said, "I am going to shower alone. As in me. Just me. Or are you going to be pushy again and not give me some space?"

"What's the matter, baby? Why so angry?"

"You are pushing too hard, too fast. I need some space. From you." She almost took back the words at his crestfallen face.

Then she tensed as she waited to see if she'd finally managed to cross a line.

The crazy lion laughed. "I'll be damned. You are getting more and more independent each day. This new assertive side of you is sexy, baby."

"It is?" Somehow she managed to ask as she gaped at him in disbelief.

"Super sexy. Makes me hot as hell too. I don't suppose I could get you to wear a cop uniform? Maybe play with some cuffs."

The heat in her face had nothing to do with embarrassment but was all about the awakening arousal making her pulse pound as she could so easily—and naughtily—picture what he said.

He took a step toward her. She took one back and held out her hand. "Stop right there. I mean it. I need some time alone." Because if he didn't leave now, they'd end up in bed, probably for the rest of the day. She freely admitted she lacked restraint around him.

"I'll go for now, baby. I could use some exercise. I hear wolf chasing is lots of fun. Or so the Instagram pics I saw seemed to indicate. The lionesses had a busy night, even if a lot of their hunting seemed to involve bars and alcohol. Apparently many of my cousins seem to think your brethren might be barflies, or is that barwolves?"

"You're going to hunt them?"

"Hell yeah. And you're going to stay right here. In this condo. No going out."

"Finally he admits that's a better plan."

"No. But until I know it's safe, I don't want you going out without me."

"Is that an order?"

"Yeah, it is." He smiled as he took a few steps and invaded her space. His hard kiss stole any retort she might have made.

Leaving her breathing a little heavy, he grabbed his pants from the floor and yanked them on, hiding his muscular legs. It was awful. And not because she couldn't admire him anymore but more because she really wanted to strip them off.

Unable to watch him any longer, she fled to the bathroom, indulging in a long shower. Really long. And cold. Real cold.

She shivered, but that was okay. Hayder would warm her up.

At any moment she expected the glass partition to slide over and for him to step in. He'd say something ridiculously him like, "I need to wash my hair," and then he'd turn into a total guy and seduce her.

Oh yeah. His hands all over my body. His cock thrusting into me. The taste of him in my mouth.

Except it didn't come to pass. Had he truly left?

She'd demanded he give her space, but she never actually expected him to listen.

No one did.

Emerging from the shower, body encased in a fluffy towel, she peeked for him in the bedroom. Mussed-up sheets, curtains pulled back, no Hayder.

She dressed quickly, matching lace panties and bra and then snug yoga pants with an almost diaphanous blouse. Barefoot, she strode into the living room. It was empty.

But the kitchen held someone.

With a swirl of blonde hair and a wide smile, Luna turned from the stove. "There you are. Just in time too for not completely burnt pancakes."

Using a plastic flipper, the edge melted into a lumpy ragged mess, Luna dropped some charred on one side, almost milky white on the other pancakes onto plates.

"What happened to the plastic spatula?"

Luna waved it. "Darned things. Always melting on me. You'd think they'd make kitchen stuff that handled cooking on high." Luna slid a plate in Arabella's direction before she waved her massacred flipper. "Have a seat. I'll grab you a coffee. That I know how to make."

Thank goodness for Keurig coffeemakers else Arabella feared what sludge she might have had to drink. The pancakes proved palatable. Barely. But, since Luna had gone to the trouble, she thought it best to gag it down with a smile and thanks. No use antagonizing the obviously crazy lioness.

And yes, she meant crazy, especially given Luna's plan. "After breakfast, we'll head over to the gym and slap you around a bit."

Having just bitten into a more powdery section of pancake, the sharp breath Arabella inhaled dusted the inside of her lungs with dry ingredients. She choked. She sputtered. Her eyes watered, and she just about fell off her stool as Luna pounded her back.

"You going to live there, wolf girl?"

Live? She certainly hoped so but had to wonder, given all the plans people had for her. "Can I ask," she said after a few sips of orange juice, "why you want to beat me?"

"To get your wolf to come out and protect you, of course. I heard about your little problem."

"How? Did Hayder tell?" She didn't think he would. She hoped he wouldn't. Harry had told anyone who listened about his defective wife. *"Stupid bitch can't even shift. I only keep her around cause she can cook."*

"As if." Luna rolled her eyes. "No, we didn't get the info from Hayder. Bloody guy growls if anyone shows too much interest in you. He's also gotten really fond of the word mine. Totally retro beast if you ask me. But I guess it's hot in a primitive way. Aunt Cecily says, once he claims you, this whole prehistoric cat-man shtick will die down."

It took Arabella a moment to filter all the information. One key point stuck out. Hayder was claiming her in public? Why instead of angering her did it warm her to her toes? She'd not agreed to anything yet. Still it tickled her to know he wasn't ashamed of admitting his feelings.

She, on the other hand, was terrified to give in to—and trust—hers.

But knowing Hayder wasn't the leak didn't answer her question. "How did you hear about my wolf?"

"Jeoff, of course. While Hayder might be tight lipped, your brother, on the other hand, hasn't stopped blabbing about you. He's been ranting and raving how it's his fault you're like this and he should have done something years ago. He's moaning he's the worst brother ever."

"It's not his fault. I made my choice. Bad as it was."

Luna nodded. "Yeah, the shit that happened to you was your fault."

Arabella recoiled.

"Hold on, I don't mean it the way you think. I mean that, yes, you did choose that life, but you certainly didn't deserve what happened to you. And you were dumb in letting pride keep you from changing that."

"I didn't want anyone to get hurt."

"You're an anyone too, Arabella." Luna's mien turned from jocular to serious as they spoke. "You mean something. And you don't deserve to be hurt. It's time you cinched your brass boobs in an eye-popping bra, pushed your shoulders back, and stuck up for yourself. It's also time for your wolf to stop hiding. And the best way to get your bitch riled up is to hurt the body."

Hair flew in wet strands stinging her cheeks as she shook her head. "It won't work. Pain is why she went away."

"Is it? I say we test that theory."

"Hayder said to stay here."

"Hayder said to stay here," Luna aped. "Since when is he the boss of you?"

"He's not, but it's safer to stay in the condo."

"It's also safer to bubble wrap yourself instead of playing sports. It's safer to drink filtered tap water than fresh from a babbling stream. But do you really want to spend your life only doing what's safe?"

Put that way, Luna had a point, but the examples she used were about mundane things, not out-of-the-ordinary situations involving control-freak Lycans with violent tendencies.

"I'm staying."

Something about the clucking and chicken strutting Luna subjected her to made Arabella snap. Was she really any safer in here than out there? Hayder thought the farm was safe and look what happened. Who was to say they wouldn't take a page from her brother's book and hire a helicopter for a daring rappel kidnapping? If Jeoff could arrange it, so could her old pack.

She eyed the balcony door then the apartment one.

Luna sensed her wavering. "Oh, come on. Worst-case scenario, some ruffians come after us and we get to kick some furball ass. I hear you're more vicious than a wolverine on speed when provoked."

"Who said that?"

"Hayder. He was quite proud too."

He bragged about her? "Not proud enough or confident enough to let me go out on my own."

"What a jerk. We should show him."

"Yeah we should." Arabella almost looked around to see who'd said it.

Before she could take back the words, Luna was dragging her from the condo. She tried to protest in the elevator, only to have Luna say, "You gonna let another man tell you what to do?"

The question stuck with Arabella as she let Luna lead her from the elevator and grab a posse of two other lionesses looking to hit the gym. Suitably surrounded, even Arabella could find no fault. Wasn't Hayder the one who claimed the women of his pride kicked butt?

Since none of them wanted to drive, they hailed a cab, which deposited them ten minutes later in front of a two-story brown-brick building. Nothing modern or chrome here. As a matter of fact, it didn't look like a gym at all, despite the small hand-painted sign that read, Lion's Athletic Club.

"How original," was Arabella's dry remark upon seeing it. "However, isn't advertising the whole lion thing everywhere kind of inviting discovery."

Luna laughed. "On the contrary. In plain sight is sometimes the best camouflage."

Out in the open, and in spite of the bodies flanking her, Arabella once again questioned the wisdom in leaving the condo. "Maybe we should have stayed in. We might have been followed."

"Good. Nothing like the present to exterminate a problem."

How fearless Luna appeared. "Aren't you afraid they might be stronger?"

"I'm afraid of lightning, but it doesn't mean I won't walk in the rain. I fear human hunters with rifles, but that doesn't stop me from running in the woods. I also fear getting a fat ass from too much cheesecake, but that never prevented me from eating the whole damn thing. You can't let fear rule you."

"No fear." Arabella took a deep breath. "Sounds so simple. I'll bet it's easy for you. You ooze confidence."

"Some of that is fake. Bluffing is a great tool." Luna winked. "Now stop stalling and get your ass inside so I can chase you around a ring."

Luna meant that quite literally.

An hour later, out of breath, and ducking the umpteenth fist from Luna, Arabella managed to huff, "Are we done yet? It isn't working."

Not entirely true. Arabella could sense her wolf side—watching in snuffling amusement as Arabella squeaked and dodged the blonde dynamo in the ring. Lucky for her, Luna didn't seem intent on actually hurting her. However, the physical exertion on her poor human body proved almost as bad.

She'd gotten out of shape as a result of her secluded lifestyle with Harry.

Someone needs one of those circle things rodents run in.

The projected image of a hamster in a wheel might have proven amusing to her inner wolf, but Arabella mentally scowled.

Some of us wouldn't be so out of breath right now if a certain furry chickenpup would come out and take over.

Silence.

But not a full retreat. Far from hiding, Arabella got the impression her other side sulked. If exertion wouldn't yank her out, then maybe insults and nagging would.

A strategy Luna seemed intent on also trying. "Here puppy, puppy. Come on out, and I'll give you a Scooby snack."

"She's partial to bacon, the maple-smoked kind."

"Gotcha. I'll add Beggin' Strips to my grocery list."

Please do.

Stupid dog treats were the equivalent of candy to a human.

"We need to take a break," Arabella panted. "We've been at this for over an hour. I need a shower and some food. Lots of food."

"But we're not done."

"You might not be. But I am."

How easily the expressing of her opinion flowed now. It wasn't just with Hayder she found the confidence to speak her mind. She was doing it with others too. And no one raised a fist.

Well, actually, Luna did, but it was for a fist

bump as she yelled, "I am going to take you out to eat the best fries and burger you've ever tasted."

"Is there lots of it?"

"Tons. It's shifter owned and operated so we get special deals. And best of all, it's only a block away and super busy. No wolves would dare accost you there. Way too public."

Wow, was Luna ever wrong.

Chapter Seventeen

"What the hell do you mean you took her out?" Hayder ranted as he paced back and forth, wearing a trail in the Berber carpeting covering the floor of the condo's onsite boardroom.

A bruised and scratched Luna, one eye turning a lovely shade of purple, hung her head in contrition. A first. "I just meant to help. I thought she could use a bit of unwinding and exercise, so I took her to the gym to work out. And it wasn't like we went alone. There was a group of us—me, Nellie, and Joan."

An adequate guard, actually. It didn't lessen Hayder's glower. "Fine, so you took precautions getting there, and yet, according to reports, she wasn't taken from the gym."

"Well, no. See, after working out, she said she was hungry, so we went to lunch. Again there was a bunch of us. I wasn't stupid. A few of the other lionesses tagged along. It should have been safe. I mean we're talking about noon on a Tuesday. Tons of freaking people, humans I might add, all around."

"And yet that didn't stop them," Arik, also present for the debriefing, mused aloud.

"Didn't stop them? Understatement. They made the bloody news," Hayder shouted, still blown away by it all. Everyone was stunned by the brazen attack on

Arabella and her guards.

Usually shifters tended to try and keep their violent retaliations out of sight. The less attention they drew, the better. No one wanted to test humanity's capacity for acceptance when it came to discovering shifters and other mythical beings lived among them.

Discretion was more than a law passed down over the centuries. It was a way of life—until now.

The brawl, centered in the area around the chip truck, could have come straight from an action movie— and that was how they were spinning it online. Forget hiding all the videos bystanders filmed. There was no stopping them, and if not for the digital replay, Hayder might not have believed how it all went down.

This was a full-on assault. No discretion or hesitation. Violent and determined best described the well-executed plan. Obviously someone had notified the Lycan groups where Arabella was. They were ready to act within minutes of her exiting the gym. The best video of the unfolding action, while grainy, was jaw dropping.

As it replayed on the large LCD screen bolted to the wall, Hayder once again couldn't prevent a macabre urge to watch. There was Arabella, surrounded, as Luna claimed, by pride ladies. A large group. A safe group under most circumstance. Lips moved as the women chatted, some lounging on the picnic tables ranged alongside the chip truck. Nothing out of the ordinary so far as they waited for their foot-long sausage and onion rings. Heads turned as several vehicles screeched to a stop by the sidewalk. From the depths of the dozen or so matching SUVs spilled guys, lots of them.

The videos didn't provide smell, but given the feral miens, and what ensured next, it wasn't hard to guess they were wolves. Wolves who swarmed the lionesses and Arabella.

While some of the thugs engaged Luna and the others—to their detriment as the ladies taught them no-means-no—yet more seemed determined to grab Arabella and drag her away.

Don't touch. Apparently his lion wasn't the only one who thought those curs needed to keep their hands to themselves.

To his delight, his baby didn't let them march her away without a fight. While she didn't turn as savage as she had the night those other wolves drew his blood, she gave a good show, thrashing and flailing, even biting. However, the numbers were stacked against her. Her petite form was overwhelmed by the bastards determined to take her.

Hoisted aloft, they carted her away from the battle to the waiting vehicles. She was swallowed by one of the black SUVs. Off it sped with her a prisoner. Away it went without leaving a clear trail to follow.

It disappeared, leaving him with nothing.

Argh.

Before people wondered if the pride's security network sucked, it should be noted all the pride members drew together quickly and formed numerous hunting parties. The wolves, with their matching SUVs, led them on a merry chase. But in the end, the lions mostly prevailed.

They netted almost all the wolves and vehicles involved in the kidnapping. Only two got away. And, of course, one of them, the vehicle holding Arabella, managed to slip through their paws.

Lucky Hayder got to study her abduction from a few cell phone camera angles. Each time he watched, his blood boiled hotter and hotter.

What surprised him was the temerity of the wolves didn't have his alpha spouting off a rant and promising to rain destruction. If one ignored Hayder, those present in the boardroom were calm, so calm Leo had yet to move from his spot on the couch where he read an actual paperback book—tree killer.

The lack of any kind of vengeance-fueled emotion irritated Hayder even more. "Why aren't you more perturbed?" Did no one understand the calamity? Arabella was gone!

Fingers still texting, Arik peered up from his cell phone. "I am actually very upset, but since you're already roaring, I figure I'll save my voice for later when we accost the stupid dogs and give them payback for their effrontery." Arik's cold smile promised death.

"I want to kill them," Hayder growled. "Rip them apart. Stomp on them. Make them wish they were the load their mother swallowed."

"Dude, that was a visual no one needed. But I'll forgive it because you're upset. I'll make sure to save you a few curs when we find them so you can work on your anger issues." A thump on his back almost sent him staggering as Leo consoled him.

"So kind of you," was his sarcastic reply.

"I know. All part of my calming personality."

Calming to Leo perhaps. Anyone else watching the big man crack his knuckles would have probably swallowed in fear and wet themselves, especially if they knew to expect a visit from the granite-hard fist.

Leo liked to fight old school, bare knuckled and with the force of a freight train behind it.

Sure glad he's on our side.

"Do we even know where they are?" Hayder

asked, a little calmer now that he knew the pride was behind him and ready to mete out punishment.

"Yup. Or at least we have a fair idea of where they're going. The full moon is tonight, and the battle for alpha and Arabella is happening at midnight in Arianrhod's Meadow."

"Isn't that smack-dab in a federal park?"

Arik nodded. "That's the one. The council deemed it a neutral spot for the fight."

A fight that still boggled the feline mind. The pride only rarely resorted to battle to decide matters. When it came to leadership, the lions and other felines used more diplomatic methods and based their choice on not just physical strength but intelligence and charisma too. They wanted a true king, not a brute to rule over them.

"If we've got the spot, then what are we waiting for?"

"Who says we're waiting. I've got cars already en route."

"You what? Why the hell aren't I in one?" Any delay could prove disastrous. Not just to Arabella but himself. He walked a thin line between sanity and primitive impulse. It wasn't just his lion pulsing under the skin asking to get out. He needed to find Arabella. He needed to ensure her safety. He needed to kill something to calm the beast pulsing just under his skin.

Arik snorted. "Why drive when we can fly? The chopper is being fueled and will be on its way to grab us shortly. They might have a head start, but we'll make up time in the air."

But would they arrive before harm befell Arabella? That was the question Hayder didn't dare to ponder too long, but that made him roar in frustration.

Hold on, baby, I'm coming.

Chapter Eighteen

The end is coming.

And she didn't even get a good last meal. Damned kidnappers snagged her before she got her lunch from the chip truck. Sob. And it smelled so good. A real bacon burger with cheddar cheese, fried onions, and a bunch of yummy condiments.

Thinking about the food didn't help her hungry tummy, but it did help distract from her situation. Dire. Yup, that one word about summed it up.

Hours since her capture and a blur of unfamiliar countryside was all that she got to see from the back seat of an SUV, a seat she got to share with a pair of leering men who should really invest in a new brand of deodorant.

Keeping her eyes open and focused proved a bit of a chore, as her brain still rattled from the blow of a well-aimed fist during the melee. The needle they'd jabbed her with, packed with a sedative, when they managed to squirrel her away in the SUV didn't help matters.

Whatever the drug they used, it proved powerful. She'd passed out. Night-night. When she regained consciousness the dashboard clock showed hours had passed. Hours, and apparently neither Hayder, nor the pride, had managed to save her.

That really didn't bode well.

Either the wolves had well and truly plotted the perfect extraction, or Hayder had decided she wasn't worth the trouble.

Then again, only a suicidal idiot would start a war on Lycan turf for a woman.

Funny, I was beginning to think he was that kind of idiot, an idiot who actually cared for me.

As the minutes passed and rescue seemed less and less likely, the men in the truck began to relax. Their brash nature reasserted itself in the form of taunts.

"Did you really think you could leave the pack?"

"My dad always said women were as dumb as sheep."

"When I win the spot of alpha, you'll beg to suck my dick."

All kinds of vile words they flung at her. None of them touched her. She hid in a cocoon, a room built inside her mind that she fled to when things got too rough, except this time she wasn't alone.

A furry shape sat in a corner.

What are you doing here?

A shaggy head tilted and perused her psychic presence. *Why are you here? Have you given up?*

Arabella gave the equivalent of a mental shrug. *What else can I do? I'm outnumbered and on our way to who knows where.*

Find a way to escape.

Escape? A derisive snort almost slipped out.

Don't give up.

Says the wolf that has been hiding for years. You're not in a position to talk. You gave up and left me alone.

Didn't give up. Went away. For your safety. You almost died. My fault. No more pain. Our alpha said to go away or he would kill you. I left to save you.

It wasn't so much words her wolf bombarded her with but a rush of feelings and thoughts. Guilt mostly. Her wolf felt guilty about what had happened to her.

And her wolf blamed herself. Her inner self thought she was the cause of all the pain. Going away was her version of apology, her way of keeping Arabella safe.

But it's not your fault. He was a mean man, and I wanted to escape too. Hiding yourself away didn't make things better.

So why was she hiding now? Hiding never helped her all those years. Ignoring the truth kept her trapped in an abusive marriage for much too long. Obeying didn't stop the slaps. Subservience didn't make things better. And yet, here she was, falling into her old habit of kowtowing to men who thought they could order her around and treat her as if she was worthless.

Why? Had she not learned? Was she really going to allow these men to harass her without saying a word?

"Enough." She murmured the word, but it didn't stop the raunchy conversation consisting of a woman's duties, most of them sexual in nature.

"I said enough." Up snapped her head as she growled the words. "You will shut your filthy mouths, or I will shut them for you."

"Big words from a little bitch. How about I shut you up with my dick instead?"

Filthy pig.

Arabella had spent many years plotting revenge. She'd just never acted upon her plans. She'd watched a lot of television shows, many of them violent. She'd read a lot of books, many of those violent too. She'd learned a few things along the way. Violent things. Things she'd never dared try.

Until now.

The rapid jab of her elbow against a larynx with all the weight she, and her irritation, could manage resulted in a satisfying crunch.

It also gave her the asked-for silence—if one ignored the rattling gasps of the dying man beside her. Of course it wasn't the crushed throat that had killed him. If tended, the injury could have healed. The broken neck, however—snap!—that proved fatal.

She turned her smile on the skinny fellow beside her who uttered a, "Holy shit!"

"I'm sorry, did you want to say something?"

The pimple-faced boy wisely shook his head and kept his lips clamped. Not so the other men in the truck.

"Why you bitch. I'm going to kill you," snarled the fellow in the front seat.

She bared her teeth in a grin more feral than pleasant. "Please do. Death is better than what you all have planned. And even nicer because I've yet to write a will, which means if you kill me then all that lovely money I have that you're craving will end up in government hands."

Apparently, keeping her alive so they could get their grubby hands on her fortune—and not incur the wrath of the Lycan Council, which had coordinated the attack to snare her—was more important at the moment than avenging their friend. A friend they stripped clean of identification and dumped in the woods, dinner for the scavengers.

Arabella thought about running during that brief stop, losing herself in the thin forest. They must have sensed it because the three men, once they disposed of their friend, converged on her, and while they didn't truly hurt her—*oh but I hurt them. Those teeth marks might need stiches*—the prick of a needle sent her sinking into black oblivion.

When next she woke, she'd gone from a truly awful situation to something out of a freaking B-movie nightmare.

I'm trapped. More than trapped, she was being presented as a sacrifice.

It seemed, during her slumber, they'd arrived at their destination. While she'd never been—being a woman and all—she'd heard of the location. Arianrhod's Meadow, the sacred open-air field smack-dab in the middle of a protected forest featuring the gnarly mother tree that legend said began all life on this continent. Located somewhere in the mountains of some national park, the large clearing was filled with fragrant clover and held just the one massive tree—a tree she was chained to. This sacred spot was where the Lycans went when important matters needed resolution and only neutral ground would do.

Look at me, so important. So special they didn't want her to miss a thing. That must explain why they felt a need to tie her to the tree, and not just tie, but chain.

Metal rattled as she yanked at her arms. However, the silver cuffs, which burned and itched the skin of her wrists, held her securely. They'd left her legs free. However, that didn't do her much good. She couldn't exactly run somewhere nor was there anyone close enough for her to kick.

The good news was she wasn't the focus of attention of the hundred or so wolves gathered. All men. And way too many for one place.

There was a reason why most male wolves lived in small packs or chose a loner lifestyle. Too much testosterone in one place always resulted in violence.

Except tonight's violence was planned. Condoned even. As she took an interest in her surroundings, Arabella noted the speaker in the center of the clover-carpeted meadow. She might never have met the man, but she could guess who he was, one of the elders who helped make the decisions on the Lycan Council. The elderly man wore only an unadorned black robe, a simple garb to shuck when the time came to set his wolf free. The hood pooled around his shoulders, revealing the thinning hair on his scalp and the uncompromising lines in his face.

As if sensing her regard, he cast a glance her way. One look at his cold, dark eyes and she knew there would be no compassion granted by him. He was old-school Lycan all the way. Had to be because only a man stuck in the olden ways would agree with this barbaric madness.

Turning from her, the councilman addressed the crowd. "Welcome to the sacred meadow, my brothers. While it has been a while since we've spilled blood in this field, a gap in leadership and a need for divine intervention has made a trial by combat necessary. But we aren't afraid of a little blood and sweat." Cheers met his words. "Even though the skirmish has not yet begun, already our precious moon goddess shines her approval on us. She stands witness for the upcoming battle for the next leader of the Northern Lakes Pack." More whistles and cheers.

What a load of crap. While she'd heard of the ritual battle for alpha, Arabella had never seen it. No woman ever did.

Lycans were still a very male-based society. They made the rules. They enforced them. Or at least they did in the packs she knew on the East Coast. But after having seen Arik's pride, she had to wonder if perhaps things were different elsewhere. She certainly hadn't been raised to think of herself as inferior. Then again, she didn't learn about pack life until her parents could hide the truth no longer.

Arabella had grown up in suburbia, a normal child of yuppie parents, normal that was until she hit her teens and the truth came out.

Waking up in the garden with vague wispy memories of chasing rabbits—and catching one, gag—led her running to her mother, the sobs and panic making her incoherent.

But her mother knew what had happened. "Darling, you're a werewolf." Funny how those words still had the power to echo with import even all these years later. Most girls got pads—with wings—when they got their period, she got a crash course in how her life would change.

Being out of the pack loop didn't mean her parents didn't teach her and Jeoff the fundamentals of pack existence. They knew of the Lycan groups, and the shifter council, as well as the laws that governed them.

Those strictures and a dislike of pack life were what had led to her parents leaving in the first place after Jeoff was born. They tried to warn her that pack life might not be a good fit, that she was better off living on the outside.

Silly Arabella thought living with her own kind sounded grand, hence another part of the reason why she'd jumped on Harry's offer of marriage.

"Marry me and come join my pack. Be with your own kind. Never hide what you are. Be with me." All the right words.

How could she say no when he promised her what she wanted? A place she could belong and be herself.

Wrong.

But there was no use lamenting over the past. Only the now counted, a now that saw men shrugging off clothes and entering the centuries-old, makeshift outdoor ring.

None of them looked at her, yet she studied them. One of these men would own her before the night was over.

It made her sick to her stomach.

I'll fight before I let anyone claim me again.

She pulled at the chains holding her, but they were no looser than before. The fighting was about to begin. The contenders lined up, and the elderly councilman announced them by name, pack, and current rank to the watching crowd. Some got cheers. Others jeers.

Each of them said the same ritual words declaring their intent. "I challenge those present for the next position of alpha."

Those vying for position of alpha ranged in age and size, from the young and smooth-skinned wiry type to the older barrel-chested fellow whom she recognized as Fergus, an alpha of a small pack in the country who'd already gone through four wives.

She couldn't help but shudder, only partially from the cold.

Night had fully fallen, and the soothing rays of the moon no longer bathed her skin, as it currently hid behind a cloud. Even if cloaked, she could feel its pull, the silvery voice that sang *Run with me. Run. Fly. Free.*

It had been years since she'd last truly heard the moon's siren song, a sign her wolf was close to the surface. Back. And just in time for the end.

With the moon not sharing its silvery glow, things were delayed as lights were installed around the perimeter. No one wanted to miss the action.

A healthy respect for the forest, and their own skin, meant the Lycans used electric torches instead of real flame ones. The evenly spaced glow of a few dozen battery-powered lanterns wasn't enough to disperse all the shadows. The large clearing boasted dark crevices and pockets of darkness around its outer edges, spots that could hide anything, like a man, with eyes of molten gold, a mien of fierce determination, shoulders wide with pride, and a swagger fit for a king.

Before anyone could react to Hayder's presence, he spoke, his voice ringing powerfully. But more astonishing was what he said.

"I challenge those present for the next position of alpha."

Chapter Nineteen

A furor of snarls, yelled denials, and rude remarks about his ancestry greeted Hayder's announcement.

It might have gone on for a while—and ended in carnage, given what one dog said about his mother. However, the outrage died down as an old fellow, sporting the latest in Grim Reaper robes, lifted his arms and uttered a single word, which echoed. "Silence." It got everyone's attention.

Cool trick, one that only true omegas could command. Leo could do the voice trick, but he preferred not to. Said he preferred a more hands-on approach. Literally.

As Hayder waited for the old dude to speak, his eyes scanned the area, even if he already knew the layout. Courageous and determined didn't mean stupid. He'd checked things out before boldly striding in. Not that there was truly much to see.

They were in the woods. No buildings or roads marked the area. Yet despite the lack of manmade items, the huge clearing, ringed by forest, appeared artificial. The lack of trees in the unexpected meadow, even saplings or bushes, seemed to indicate some kind of grooming, and yet, if it was manmade, then whoever maintained it managed to keep a wild, untamed essence to the spot.

The rich clover covering the ground in a soft green carpet emitted a fragrant aroma that tickled his nose. If this wasn't a life-or-death situation, he might have enjoyed a nice roll in the lush ground mattress, but it was hard to think about the simple pleasures when Arabella hung chained to a gigantic, half-dead tree.

Chained.

To a fucking tree.

He'd almost gone furry at the sight, especially when he realized they'd bound her with silver.

They dare to hurt our mate?

The temerity boggled his mind—and blew his lion's. As Hayder let his gaze stray her way, he almost lost it again. Fucking chained. Like an animal.

Did they not know who she was?

The most important thing in the world.

My mate. My baby.

Keep it cool. Keep it calm. He couldn't afford to let mindless rage control his actions. Lucky for him, a certain omega named Leo had taught him some techniques to rein in his wilder impulses.

Breathe in and focus on an object. Breathe out, stayed focused. Breathe in, focus on an object—*like that dude, the big one with the scraggly excuse for a beard, sneering on the end. He dies first.* Breathe out. Breathe in. *Need a second focus for after I kill the first one. How about his buddy beside him?*

Keeping his eyes away from Arabella, whose expression he couldn't read given the shadows, he chose to listen instead as the omega wolf, here on behalf of the Lycan Council, spoke to the crowd in general.

"A challenge has been placed. The Lycan Council recognizes the challenge and accepts it."

One voice dared to yell with evident disbelief. "What the fuck, man? He's a goddamn lion. He ain't allowed to challenge for the pack."

Murmurs erupted, and heads nodded all around. The curs thought they knew the laws.

Wrong.

Hayder allowed himself a tight smile. "Shall you tell them, old man, or shall I?"

Omega or not, the council dude shot him an irritated glare. "Don't push it, cat." The robed fellow turned to face the crowd. "Unfortunately, he is allowed. In a regular pack challenge, where the next alpha is chosen from within, outsiders aren't allowed. However, since we made this an open challenge to bring in new blood, then the law clearly states any who wish to enter may do so by declaring themselves. Even if they're not a male wolf. It is a loophole that, while discussed, was never actually closed."

Because the Lycans never could agree to anything without a fight. In this case, Hayder thanked them for their idiocy.

"Unfair," shouted a voice.

"Unfair?" Hayder's brows rose in a querying note. "Is this your way of declaring all these fine men vying for pack alpha are too weak to prevail against a single lion?" He smiled—and yes, he made sure it was mocking.

Teeth gnashed, foreheads furrowed, and a low grumble arose, but there was no further argument about him competing.

"Do any others wish to contend?" the old fellow asked.

No one in the crowd stepped forth. Those who wanted to win the position of alpha already stood in the center of the clearing.

But wait. One more voice wanted to be heard.

"I challenge those present for the next position of alpha."

Snickers immediately arose as Arabella's challenge was submitted. Heckles and ridicule immediately followed.

"You can't be alpha. You're a girl," yelled one fellow.

"You can dominate me any time," said another with a leer. As he was one of the fighters vying for alpha, Hayder made a note to kill him first. *Leer after my woman, will he?*

"I demand my right to challenge." Despite being tied to a tree, she managed to sound quite determined, her voice barely wobbling, and yet, she had to be terrified.

However, she shouldn't fear. After all, he had arrived to the rescue, just like a gallant knight—one with great hair.

Sharp teeth. His lion saw their good attributes in a different light.

To Hayder's surprise, the old fellow accepted her claim. "A challenge has been placed. The Lycan Council recognizes the challenge and accepts it."

"Untie me then."

The old fellow let a sly smile crease his lips. "No. While you can challenge, the rules don't say we have to release you to do so. Challenges are come as is."

And as is for her was a sacrificial hottie who, instead of dropping her head in defeat, threw daggers with her eyes.

So sexy. But now wasn't the time to get distracted. Time to be a hero. "Are we going to get this show on the road? I've got rabbits to chase. A woman to claim. A pack to own."

More than a few growls met his taunting words.

Being a bit of a smartass, Hayder made a 'come and get me' gesture with his fingers. He laughed when no one stepped forth.

Dude in the robes raised his arms in the air, the sleeves of his outfit sliding down to reveal skinny arms. But a slight body didn't mean a tiny voice. The old guy omega-ed his next words so they fairly boomed. "Contenders, pair off. As you all know, there are only two rules. Fights are to be one-on-one. No teaming up and no weapons apart from you or your beast. Killing and maiming is allowed."

"Don't forget to tell them that cowards and cry babies may crawl off the field at any time to forfeit." Hayder grinned as he flexed his shoulders.

The omega spat out the last part of his speech while glaring. "Last one standing shall be the new alpha of the Northern Lakes Pack."

Rawr.

Okay, so Hayder was a little excited—and he just couldn't hide it! Then again, roaring was never a bad thing, as it tended to freak out his opponents. It was one thing to knowingly go into a fight against someone of your species, but throw in a giant cat, with an impressive mane, smooth coat, razor-sharp claws, and determination? Yeah, the dogs knew they were in trouble.

Not a man to hide from danger, Hayder paired himself against the biggest contender. The bastard who'd leered at his woman.

Muscles bunched, eyes locked, and opponents prepared themselves.

The signal was simple. The old guy dropped his arms.

As Hayder dove into the skirmish, fists flying and connecting, he spent a quick second mentally thanking Arik who had the foresight to fly them in.

The chopper Arik had chartered had grabbed them from the condo's rooftop, and while it did need to stop and refuel on the way, it made good time. Real good, which meant they could afford the inconvenience of being deposited a few miles out so that the lions, and one wolf brother who'd hitched a ride, could approach on foot with stealth as their ally.

Unfortunately, the caravan of cars and trucks hadn't yet arrived, a major accident on the highway having delayed them.

It meant that there was only a half-dozen of them against a hundred or so. Challenging odds, or as Arik, the spoilsport, declared when they were plotting in the woods, "Fucking suicide. We'll have to wait until the others arrive."

Wait? Hayder wasn't about to wait, and lucky for him, Jeoff had just the stalling tactic he needed.

"We can't wait. I've got a plan. I'll challenge for alpha." A simple solution offered by Jeoff.

A solution Hayder tweaked to suit himself.

Originally, Jeoff planned to be the one to throw his hat into the ring, or was that put his left paw in, his left paw out, his left paw in and shake it all about?

However, Hayder wasn't about to let him get the glory. *I'm going to save my baby.*

As to what he'd do if, hold on, make that when, he won? He'd always wanted a pet growing up. Now he could have a whole pack.

The big dude he battled handled the first few

smacks to his face with hardly a wince. The wrench of his head? Judging by the crack, not so well.

On to the next opponent. And the next.

It soon became apparent that, while teaming up wasn't allowed, a certain cheat was taking place. None of the contending wolves were fighting each other. Nope, they lined up and waited their turn to attack Hayder.

Taken on one at a time, he didn't worry about losing. He was more than a match for these bastards. What did worry him was fatigue. By the sixth fellow, Hayder tired. He slowed. As his strength waned, so did his speed. His opponents managed to land a few blows. This was where his hard head came in handy. *See, Mom, it turned out to be a good thing.*

Lucky for him, he got a bit of respite once he'd finished off the first half of the men who fought him.

The old dude shouted, in a tone that resonated, "Challengers, you've shown your worth as a man. Now time to show your worth as a beast. All remaining participants for the alpha position shift."

Fingers quickly tore clothes from the body. It didn't take long since most had entered the battle ring clad only in shorts or pants.

Hayder made quick work of sliding his own trousers down. It took even less time to coax his lion forward. Adrenalized and eager, his feline bounded forward and took the driver's seat to his body. Hayder breathed through the pain of the change then exulted in it because, as the agony of the morph faded, his senses sharpened. Strength returned to him.

An eagerness for battle infused him.

Lots of wolves to play with.

Rawr!

Chapter Twenty

Rawr.

While Arabella's oral exclamation might not have the timbre or weight of a lion's roar, it did aptly express her frustration.

Tied to a tree, a victim again. "Let me go," she yelled in vain. No one in the crowd paid her any mind. She was beneath their notice. A mere woman.

A woman whose man risked all to save her.

To save me. Because I can't save myself.

How many more times was she going to let people make choices for her? When would she stand up for herself? A few days ago, Arabella had thought she was powerless, that her only option was to hide. But hiding wasn't a life. She had the right to choose her future. She didn't have to let others make that choice for her.

She was allowed to fight.

What of the pain that comes from defiance? Her wolf whispered the thought to her, but for once, Arabella didn't let it quell her spirit.

What of the pain? She'd tried subservience. She'd tried ducking low. It didn't stop the blows. Her meek attitude didn't halt the disgusting words, or the shame. If submitting wasn't working, then why was she allowing them to cow her? Would she stand and do nothing while others fought her battles?

Hell no.

When the Lycan elder asked if anyone else wished to fight, she surprised everyone by announcing her intent.

It had been accepted. Yay.

Of course, she did have a slight problem in that she was kind of tied up at the moment.

She let out a groan of frustration.

"Hold your Kibbles and Bits," grumbled a familiar female voice. "Do you have any idea how hard it is to sneak up on a group of wolves when the damned wind keeps switching directions."

"Luna, what are you doing here?" Arabella whispered, keeping her gaze on Hayder so as to not give the lioness away.

"Doing? Rectifying a mistake. Apparently, I should have taught you how to escape handcuffs before how to get out of a chokehold."

"You should go. If they catch you—"

"Don't start with the I'm-not-worth-the-help crap again."

"I wasn't going to. I was going to say if they catch you, you'll probably end up with blood on your new T-shirt."

Luna snickered. "Cold water will take care of that. No worries. Now hold still for a second, and I'll have you out of those cuffs in a jiff."

True to her word, Luna didn't fiddle long before Arabella felt more than heard a click. Hard to hear when the crowd of watching Lycans cheered as Hayder tired.

The first half of the match was done. Now came the second part, beast to beast. Seven opponents left.

Hayder's lion stood golden and gorgeous. A

lethal machine with the softest mane.

Arms free, Arabella took a step from the tree, but not in the direction of freedom. Despite Luna tugging at her, Arabella couldn't move. Fascinated, she watched as her leonine lover showed the deadly stealth and killer abilities of his kind.

He didn't just dominate in size. He outclassed the wolves with bite and dexterity of the paws. With his claws he could swipe and hook a wolf. Once he yanked his opponent to the ground, his jaw clamped around the neck. Crunch. As one went down, another stepped in.

He was winning. Killing. But as before, after the fourth opponent, his movements slowed. His lion tired. A slash of red appeared on a shoulder as a wolf managed a chomp.

Wince.

More blood flowed as teeth tore at his front leg.

Gasp.

Injured or not, Hayder wouldn't give up.

He fights for me. He fights for us. Are you going to let this happen? Are you going to keep hiding? She addressed the watching presence of her wolf.

As Hayder staggered, and another wound opened, the blood flowing in red sluggish lines, the leash holding her wolf prisoner snapped. *No more!*

Her wolf snarled as she burst free. Clothes shredded, skin pulsed and rippled as fur sprouted.

Arabella emitted an ecstatic scream as the pain of the change swept her. At long last she was one again with her wolf.

They were united in body. Spirit. And rage.

They hurt our mate.

Then let's hurt them back.

Only one contending wolf remained in the ring

with the exhausted lion. The nastiest one. Fergus, a man with slabs of muscle, and a wolf that peeled back its lip to show pointed canines.

On four paws, she ran to the bloody field of battle, only to stop short instead of diving in.

She retained enough of her wits to know she couldn't interfere. The laws allowed only one challenger at a time. If she tried to help him now, everything Hayder had sacrificed was for naught, not to mention, if she interfered, their lives would be forfeit.

Unless her tired lover conceded and let her finish this.

She tried to catch his eye, to convey her intent. *Let me fight.*

I'm a woman. He'll never let me. He'll nev—

With a might bat of his paw, Hayder hobbled the grizzled wolf. Before Fergus could regain his feet, Hayder walked away, tail swishing.

She stared at him. They all did.

Fergus, the last wolf left standing, let out a howl of triumph.

She cut it short when she slammed into him.

This fight isn't done.

As she grappled with the wolf, she had a moment to wonder what the hell she was doing, especially when the other wolf managed to nip her in the shoulder.

But the pain didn't send her into a paralyzed panic, nor did she submit.

Those days were over.

I won't be a victim again. Of course that decision would work a lot better if she'd not stupidly challenged a full-sized male wolf.

I can't do this.

So she thought. But Hayder seemed to think otherwise.

"Come on, baby. You can do this. He's old and tired. Go rabid on his ass so we can finish this and go for dinner."

I'm trying to, dammit.

"I hear there's a twenty-four-hour diner that serves a juicy burger, homemade fries, and a killer Black Forest cake."

Tempting, but it didn't give her the extra fifty pounds she needed to truly take on Fergus. She twisted and avoided a pinning grip by the other wolf, but she was on the defensive. Not good.

"They've got rooms we can rent, too, with hot showers."

Mmm. Naked time with her mate? She narrowly avoided getting pinned.

"Maybe you could kiss my booboos better. That mean old wolf hurt me."

A wounded mate?

Snap.

As before, she didn't truly recollect what she did. She just got to see the aftermath. It wasn't pretty, left her messy, but it was effective.

She was the last wolf standing.

We won. We fucking won.

Her wolf emitted a joyous howl that rang through the silent clearing. It seemed those present were in a state of shock.

As she changed shapes, Hayder strode toward her, naked and tempting. She finished morphing in time for his exuberant whoop and twirl as he grabbed her around the waist and swung her.

"You did it, baby. You're the new alpha."

"Like hell," snarled the elder, who glared at them both.

"Rules are rules," Hayder taunted. "She challenged, you accepted, she won."

The Lycan councilor was past listening. Splitting skin, he shed his robe and let his gray wolf out to play.

He bounded at them, jaws wide, a slavering beast, and yet Hayder didn't budge. He simply tucked her into his side, and when the old wolf leaped, he grabbed him by the furry throat. He held the wolf in the air. The muscles in his arm bunched as he strained.

"Is this the kind of honor wolves have?" He shook the beast, who, of course, couldn't answer, unless *grrr* counted.

With a tsk of disapproval, Hayder flung the wolf in the direction of the crowd. The Lycan councilmember landed with a yelp. When he stood, it was on three legs, the hind one held off the ground.

Injured and bested didn't mean he'd accepted defeat. He let out an ululating howl, a howl repeated as everyone left in the field adopted their canine side and turned baleful eyes their way.

A violent tension filled the air, as did howls and snarls of challenge.

Uh-oh.

For a moment, a flutter of fear threatened. Arabella trembled but only for a second before her jaw dropped in stunned disbelief as the woods suddenly erupted with feline roars...

And golden fury.

The rest of the pride had arrived, and they were ready to fight.

Hayder laughed. "Betcha those Lycans weren't expecting that."

Nope, but even better, they were too busy fighting the pride's army to bother her and Hayder.

She placed her hands on his chest and peered at his face. "I can't believe you came for me."

"Of course I did. I wasn't letting one of these bastards claim you."

"Thank you. I appreciate that."

"You can thank me when I claim you later." He winked.

He still meant to mate her? She let him off the hook. "You don't have to claim me anymore. While I was tied to the tree, I came up with a plan to get them to leave me alone. First thing tomorrow, I'm going to make Jeoff the manager and beneficiary of my assets. " It was what she should have done in the first place once she realized the packs were all after her money.

"Even if you're poor, you're still alpha of the pack now. People will want your job. You need someone to watch your back."

"Which is why I'll have Jeoff as my beta. He can handle enforcement for the pack."

"Leaving you free and clear."

"Exactly. So, you needn't give up your life for me."

"Baby, I am not claiming you as some sort of cure for your problems. I'm a lion. I'm selfish. Claiming you is all about me because I want you. All to myself."

"Even if we're different?"

"Because we're different. Because you're awesome. What do you say? Will you—"

A furry body took that moment to interrupt, slamming into Hayder and sending her reeling.

"Do you mind?" bellowed Hayder as he quickly regained his feet and took on the interrupting wolf.

Tired, but not afraid, Arabella sat down on the soft clover, a spot not marked by blood, and watched. While the lions were clearly outnumbered, they still prevailed. They also showed mercy.

While some furry bodies lay on the field, never to rise again, most limped off into the shadows of the woods, leaving to lick their wounds and conceding the impromptu war to the lions.

While the moon might traditionally belong to the wolves, that didn't stop the pride's felines from setting up a chuffing sound, a victory song of sorts.

From the gathered golden bodies, one separated itself, his golden nimbus of hair framing his head, his amber eyes fixed on her. With majestic steps, Hayder came strutting, and when he drew alongside, she didn't need to see the tilt of his head to understand what he wanted.

She clambered onto his back, burrowing her face in his mane, holding him tight and letting him carry her from the battleground.

A rumble overhead seemed almost conjured. How propitious that the rain would come to wash away the violence lest human authorities come across it.

Of course, while she welcomed the sluicing water, which rinsed the blood from her skin, Hayder let out a rumble of discontent as his fluffy mane soaked up the moisture and flattened.

The mini storm ended before they reached the pride vehicles located in a lot on the outskirts of the park. Once they got there, she slid off Hayder's back and couldn't hold in a giggle when Hayder switched back to his man shape.

"Something funny, baby?"

She pointed and snickered. "Your hair is curly."

"Stupid rain," he grumbled as he tried to finger comb and flatten the curling wisps.

As Hayder rummaged in the trunk of a truck, she couldn't help but yawn and then sneeze as Hayder handed her a shirt that smelled of him.

To his credit he didn't sigh loudly when she went into a mini fit, but he did threaten to shave Luna's head if she didn't stop laughing.

Not cowed at all, Luna replied, "Touch my hair and I'll Nair you while you sleep."

The banter of the lions that rode with them in the large Suburban lulled Arabella to sleep on Hayder's lap. He claimed he held her so there'd be enough room for everyone. The fact that they ended up with the back seat to themselves didn't change his stance. She remained on his lap, cuddled in his arms, and drooling on his shirt when she fell asleep, mouth open because her sinuses were stuffy again.

When the vehicle stopped and Hayder slid out of the backseat, still holding her in a firm grip, she woke but told her newly discovered independent streak to take a hike for the night. She liked this gallant side of Hayder. He treated her like something precious, and she, for one, intended to enjoy it.

It seemed arrangements had already been made with the motel because Hayder produced a keycard and let them into a room on the ground floor.

He didn't set her down until he'd kicked the door closed, but even then, he kept his arms loosely looped around her.

"Hop into bed, and I'll tuck you in," he murmured.

Bed? No way. She wasn't that tired anymore, not now that they'd finally gotten somewhere private, with a bathroom. "I need a hot shower."

She didn't bother to extend him an invite. She trusted her striptease as she sashayed toward the only door in the room would prove enticement enough. It was.

As she was bent over the tub, turning on the faucet and triggering the pin to get the showerhead going, he came up behind her.

Naked.

Very naked, and aroused.

His hands burned the skin of her hips where he placed them. The molten length of his shaft pressed against the crease of her buttocks. When she straightened, she leaned back into him, loving the solid strength of his chest at her back, the soft brush of his lips across the top of her head, the sensual slide of his hands across her stomach.

"Now that we're alone, am I allowed to admit I was scared?" His words surprised her.

"You? Scared? Of what? You clearly outmatched those men."

He spun her in his arms. "Bah. I wasn't scared of those fools. I was scared for you. When I realized they had you…" He cupped her chin in his hand, his thumb stroking her cheek. "I don't know if I could handle losing you."

His admission triggered one of her own. "I don't think I could handle losing you either. I've become a little fond of you."

"Only a little?" he teased.

An impish smiled curled her lips. "What was I thinking using the term little? Nothing about you is little." She curled her hands around his length and squeezed it.

He sucked in a breath. "And to think I thought you were shy."

"Not shy. Just hiding. But I'm done with that. Say hello to the new, bolder me." The new bolder her tugged him by the dick until he clambered into the shower with her. The warm water sluiced their skin, rinsing them, but even better, it made him slick.

She craned on her tiptoes for a kiss, meshing her lips to his in a hot fusion of passion while her hand gripped and stroked his erection.

Their tongues dueled for dominance, and while no clear winner emerged, it left them both aroused and panting.

His hands cupped her bottom, his callused thumbs stroking the skin and sending jolts of awareness zinging through her. But this time wasn't going to be just about her.

For a selfish lion, Hayder had given quite a bit of himself to her. He gave her pleasure. He gave her understanding. He helped her find her true self. The real Arabella. Now she wanted to give something back.

She dropped to her knees and brought herself eye level with his shaft.

He groaned even before she brought her mouth close. "Baby, what are you doing?"

She answered by taking the rounded head of his cock into her mouth and sucking. A nice long suck. A tremor went through him, and his fingers threaded through her damp hair.

She took him deeper, suctioning his length, reveling in the steel-wrapped-in-velvet skin. Everything about Hayder was strong. Including his desire for her.

Guess what, though, her need was just as powerful.

She spent a few minutes on her knees, pleasuring him with her mouth, bringing him to the edge, feeling him pulse in her mouth. When he got too close, she stopped, drew back, and blew on him, soft puffs of air that still made him shudder.

As she worked his long cock, her hands kneaded his sac, massaging it and rolling it through her fingers until he growled in warning, "Baby."

I think I've tortured him, tortured us both, enough.

She stood and meshed her mouth to his, even as his hands spanned her waist and he hoisted her. Against the cool tile wall he leaned her, the fever of her skin not quelled at all but, rather, enhanced.

He drew his hips back, far enough that the head of his cock nudged at her sex. Wrapping her legs around his waist, she drew him to her and, in doing so, sheathed him into her body.

He let out a long sigh as his molten length sank deep, and she couldn't help but make a sound herself, a rumble of pleasure as her channel tightened around him.

Together, they rocked and ground their hips together, not quite thrusting, but who needed a hard pounding when he could swirl and push and grind against her? Whatever the motion, the angle and his length meant delicious friction within, a tapping of a spot she'd thought myth.

She clawed at his shoulders as the tension within her built. And built. All her muscles tightened, especially her sex. The quiver of her channel proved too much for him.

He groaned as he shoved as deep as he could and held himself there, held himself within her as his hot seed spilled. The pulsing of his cock was enough to trigger her own orgasm.

She cried out his name as she came. "Hayder."

He groaned, and as she pulsated around his shaft, he withdrew and slammed back. In and out. In and out, drawing out her orgasm and building it again at the same time.

However, it was his whispered, "Mine," just before he clamped his teeth on the soft flesh of her shoulder that made her come again—and while in the throes, she bit him back.

Claimed.

Joined.

Forever.

But she wasn't afraid of commitment. Not afraid to live. Not anymore. Not ever again.

Epilogue

It was a week after the whole wolf challenge fiasco, and the pride had made its way back home where a celebration ensued. They celebrated victory. They toasted their beta's new claimed status. They fist pumped Arabella's victory over the wolves.

Poor Arabella, though, didn't get to keep her alpha status for long. The Lycan Council, rather than face the embarrassment of having a woman lead a pack, disbanded it and sent its member off to merge with other groups.

Not that Arabella cared because, as she claimed, "There's better shopping around here."

The attacks on her stopped after the battle, and to ensure they wouldn't resume, Hayder made it known that he'd not only claimed her sweet ass—in every position, room, and way possible—but that she'd also written a will leaving her entire fortune, in the case of her demise, to a charity that helped battered women rebuild their lives.

However, these precautions didn't mean Hayder wasn't vigilant. He'd found something precious in Arabella, and he never wanted to see it come to harm.

As Arabella towel dried her hair, Hayder grabbed his body spray and spritzed. Head to toe.

Achoo! Achoo! Achoo! Achoo!

On and on she went while Hayder stared at his spray then her. When she finally stopped, red eyed, with a towel pressed to her face, he couldn't wait to tell her the news.

"Baby, you're not allergic to me. Well, you are, but not really. It's the body spray!" Shaking the bottle, he grinned.

She glared.

He grinned wider and totally didn't flinch when she growled and punched him. Any show of spirit was cause for celebration. As she stalked from the bathroom, he admired beauty of her heart-shaped ass before tossing the spray into the trashcan. He'd have to switch to a different brand and get all his stuff washed because he'd wager traces of his signature scent clung to the fabric in his place.

But he'd do it, and soon too. Anything for his baby.

He delayed following Arabella, jumping into the shower so he could scrub the offending scent from his skin. When he emerged, wet and squeaky clean, he went looking for her.

Utterly naked and gorgeous, she sat on a stool eating some crispy bacon from a breakfast tray sent up from the pride's kitchen.

Before he could steal a piece, she growled. "Don't touch my bacon."

"Or else?"

She spun on the stool, fast and smooth. In a single heartbeat, she had her hand clamped around his dick.

This was promising.

"If you eat my bacon, I won't use you for dessert." She gave him a squeeze.

"But if I eat it, you'll punish me. And since you're naked, and I'm naked…" He waggled his brows.

She laughed, a free and pure sound that never failed to enchant him. He hoped to hear it a lot in the future, and he looked forward to seeing more of the teasing in her eyes and the smirk on her lips.

Arabella had found her wolf, and her pride. She'd also discovered one other important thing. "I'm so glad I met you."

"Of course you are. Which is why you're going to marry me and live happily ever after."

"Did it ever occur to you to ask instead of tell me?"

"No." Asking meant giving her a chance to say no, and he'd already booked them a honeymoon on a tropical beach—a topless one, *rawr!*

"If we're going to get married—"

"What do you mean if?" he protested. "We're already mated."

"Yes, but marriage is a legal and binding contract, which means we should have some ground rules."

"Are you dictating to me, baby?"

"I am totally"—she stroked her hand back and forth on his shaft—"dick-tating to you. Are you listening?"

Uh. What? Dammit. He tried to focus. "Listening and obeying. Your wish is my command." Maybe she'd wish for some oral. He loved to lap at her cream.

"Rule one. Don't touch my bacon. Or chocolate. Or basically anything I'm eating or might want to eat."

"Hold on, does this mean I can't masturbate

anymore? Because we both know you like eating that."

How he loved her red cheeks. "Hayder!" And the shocked tone. Even better, he smelled her arousal.

"So was that a yes or a no on the whole touching myself thing?"

Her answer was a growl as she pounced on him. He caught her with ease but still allowed himself to stumble back until his legs hit the couch. He dropped down onto it, with her on his lap. Straddling him.

He reached to brush her dark hair back, his gaze caught by the serious expression in hers.

"I'll give you my heart and soul for whatever thought is running through your head." Screw a penny. Go big or go home.

"I was thinking how much my life has changed."

"For the better of course."

She laughed. "Of course. As if your ego would allow for anything else."

"I'd do anything for you, baby." Including walking away from the fight for pack alpha so that she could realize she didn't need him or anyone else to win her battles.

"I know you would. Oh, what the hell, I'll marry you. And I'll even share my bacon because you know what? I love you."

Good thing he was already sitting. She definitely stole the strength from him in that moment. Felled the mighty lion with words.

And he had fallen, hard and fast, for the brave woman who'd gone through so much and now came out of her shell, still fragile in some ways but strong as hell in others.

Together, as a team, he'd show her how to battle the demons that haunted her. They'd take on the world.

As mates, they'd share a grand love and passion that would bring her happiness for the rest of their lives, and woe to anyone who dared to interfere.

We'll tear their heads off.

Rawr.

*

A few weeks later...

"Heads up! Or is that heads down?"

Thunk.

Either way it didn't matter. Leo caught the Frisbee with his noggin, which, given he was in the lobby of the condo complex, didn't impress him one bit. Some might have acted on that irritation—like gone after the Frisbee tosser and scalped her. Others would have engaged in an unladylike tussle. But as the pride's omega, he had a certain standard to adhere to. Leo let the irritation roll off his really wide—so wide the college football coach almost cried when he wouldn't play—shoulders.

He kept walking toward the elevator, which happened to be where the purple disc landed.

An unfamiliar scent—feline and delicious—surrounded and then brushed past him as a woman skipped past him, intent on the Frisbee. The blonde, whom he didn't recognize, stooped over to grab the plastic disk, her cropped athletic shorts molding every curve of her made-for-gripping ass and nibble-worthy thighs.

Everything about her was big, bold, and luscious.

Yummy. And it wasn't just his inner beast that

thought so.

Who is this delicious handful? He didn't recall meeting her, and he certainly wouldn't have forgotten her.

The unknown woman straightened and faced him, and by face him, he meant almost eye to eye, which was unheard of, given he was close to seven feet. Yet this woman, with the wicked curves, must have stood at least six foot one or a touch more.

She wasn't dainty, not by any stretch, not with the way her impressive breasts strained at her T-shirt, distorting the cartoon on it that said, Delicate Freakn' Flower. Her indented waist was accented by the flair of her hips. The quirk of her lips matched the mirth in her eyes.

While not a man prone to strong emotion, Leo was suddenly possessed of a powerful urge to drag this woman into his arms and...do decadent things that would get even his steady heart racing.

"Well, hello there, big fellow. I don't think we've met."

Indeed they hadn't, or he would have remembered her—and remembered to avoid her because anyone could see by the saucy tilt to her hips and the appraising look in her eye that she spelled trouble.

Leo didn't do trouble. He preferred calm moments. Serene outings. Quiet evenings. Very quiet. A quiet she disrupted with her Frisbee antics, so he took her to task. "You're not supposed to play Frisbee inside. It's one of the association rules." He'd know. He'd helped draft them. Leo liked rules, and he expected people to follow them. When any group of predators lived in close proximity, keeping hot tempers under control was important, hence his job to enforce the rules and keep the peace.

"No playing inside either?" Her lower lip jutted. "Do you know I got in trouble by a nice policeman for playing on the street? If I can't play inside and I can't play outside, where is a girl supposed to play?"

Upstairs, eleventh floor, condo unit 1101. His bedroom had plenty of room. Of course, the sport he pictured didn't involve any props. Nor did it include any clothes. But telling her she could play with him naked probably wasn't the answer she looked for. "We don't play in the city. Not enough room. That's what the ranch is for."

"Ah, the farm. That place still around? Awesome."

"You know of it?" He frowned. While not a closely guarded secret, only approved shifters were allowed on the property. "Who are you? I don't think I've seen you around before."

"Yeah, it's been a while since I visited. That's what happens when a girl gets banned for a few years because of a silly misunderstanding."

Banned? Wait a second. He did know who this was. He'd heard Arik say something about a cousin on his father's side visiting for a bit. She needed to hide out while some kind of scandal blew over. "You're that troublemaker from out West, aren't you?"

"Me, a troublemaker? No, that's my sister, Teena. I'm Meena, her twin, more commonly known as catastrophe. But you can call me your mate."

And with that, she flung herself on him and planted a big, juicy smooch on his lips.

The End...

...of Hayder and Arabella's story, but the fun continues in A Lion's Pride series with Leo's story, , *When an Omega Snaps.*

Author's Note:

Thank you so much for reading my lion story. I had so much fun writing it as I adore furry heroes that *roar*! If you have a moment, I would love it if you left a review. To check out more of my books, please visit my website at EveLanglais.com.

Thank you for reading.

~ Eve Langlais

CPSIA information can be obtained at www.ICGtesting.com
Printed in the USA
LVOW06s0533050915

452973LV00014B/596/P

9 781514 109335